AF504981

The
COVER
GIRL
Uncovered

By Rhona Rabble

The Cover Girl

Uncovered

Copyright © Aileen Russell 2021

All Rights Reserved.

This book is a work of fiction. Any references to historical events, real people or real locales are used fictitiously. Other names, characters places and incidents are the product of the authors' imagination, and resemblances to actual events or locals or persons, living or dead are entirely coincidental.

All intellectual rights and property are reserved

www.theloneswift.com

Contents

Catch Me If You Can

The gunfire raged over head. Nicholas kept his head down below the wall and waited for the moment to make his move. When the enemies paused to reload, he stood up, gun raised and with three clean shots he took them down. The bangs echoed round the street leaving an eerie silence in their wake. He walked over to the bodies and pull out the memory stick. The silence was cut as more shots was fired over his head. Right at that second his phone rang. Glancing at the screen and aiming a couple of shots round the corner he read "Brady" on the screen.

"Now is not a great time Brady," Nicholas yelled down the line over the fresh bangs and rolled behind a wall narrowly missing a bullet. Dust sprinkled into his hair as he peaked over the top.

"Hey Nicholas, I hope you are having a pleasant time." Brady replied lazily down the phone. She worked in the intelligence office and had recently been promoted to head communication and electronic mission handling.

"What do you think?" he asked, vaulting over a wall, dashing to the nearest building to get access to the roof. He heard a buzzing overhead as a drone flew down next to him, a camera pointing right at him. "Brady, you need to stop hacking the drones for your own personal use." He could see the gunman on the other side of the street moving to a better position.

"I'm designed this, I'm testing it out. Look I've got a date with Harry tonight. Do you think I should tell him what my real job is? He's started to ask annoying questions." She asked as if they were having a heart to heart in a coffee shop. Nick fired more shots and mad an exasperated noise down the phone. He could hear her laughing as he pulled the speaker away to return fire. The next bullets missed him by inches, causing his frustration to grow.

"Brady this isn't the time to discuss this." Nick yelled throwing himself to the ground out of the way of a huge explosion.

"For god's sake hang on," She replied impatiently. The drone whirled away and shot the man down at point blank range. The street fell quiet again and the drone hovered next to Nicholas. "Right, now what do you think?" Nick gave the finger to the drone. "Rude!" said Brady laughed at him, making the drone follow him as he moved out of his cover spot. Before anyone else came it was time to move on to the next phase of the mission.

"Look if you want to tell him, just do it, but make sure you get him to sign an NDA in case you break up." Nick said as he reached the car and jumped in. It took a moment to hot wire it and he skidded off through the dusty streets. The drone buzzed along overhead following him and scanning the area.

"I think he might be the one. It's been two years now," Brady said dreamily down the phone. She reminded him of Alex when she spoke like that although the two only met in person for a few days. Nick put on a serious voice.

"Look life it too short to keep secrets. You realise that in this job. Tell him, if he loves you then he will forgive you. Easy as that." Nick said seriously looking at the drone. A message popped up on his phone and he pulled it away from his ear to look at the new assignment. Nick blinked at the screen nearly crashing the car. "Brady, are you seeing this?" He shoved his foot down on the break and stops dead in the middle of the road, all thought of escape leaving his mind.

"Hang on," she said and I hear the clicking through the speaker phone. "New target," she read, "Wanted under suspicion of fraud." Brady fell silent. Staring back out of the screen is the exact double of Alex Shaw. "Name unknown. Could it be her?" Brady asks as Nick remained silent as the shock passed. The same glint in her eye, same scar on her cheek but her hair was different. She looked scared.

"It's her, she's alive." Nick said under his breath. He grasped for the key to start the engine up again not taking his eyes off the screen. "Brady, tell the office I'm taking on the assignment and I am on my way back to New York. I need to have a word with Walter."

****

The board room was full when Nick entered fresh off the plane from the middle east. Brady was there to meet him at the door and handed him a file. The stood at the end of the room as the FBI meeting began.

"Here is the target," said the officer delivering the brief. A picture of Alex from years ago appeared on the projector. "This is the infamous Cover Girl who operated in London until her death last year. But we believe that her death was faked and has been continuing her work undercover." The slide clicked onto various pictures of her in disguise. There were only a handful of pictures. "These orders have come from the president himself. I cannot emphasise in the world situation how important it is to find this woman." Nick rolled his eyes at this and was noticed by the leader.

"Do you have an opinion on the matter Mr Castle, she was after all your primary protection when you worked with MI5 in

London." The leader addressed him and the entire room looked round to see his reaction.

"No mam," he said, keeping his head down reading the file. "But I saw Miss Shaw's body. Are we sure that this is not another criminal who has taken on her alias? Her reputation was world renowned after all."

"We have confirmed genetic analysis of a blood sample that was left at a scene. Miss Shaw is very much alive." The leader replied which caused a stir throughout the room. Nick ran his hand through his hair taking in a deep breath as the officer continued but Brady interrupted him with a thought.

In the last few months, he had been thinking off her. He had rescued an agent from a burning building he had never heard off. He had imagined her in the street but when he caught up with the woman it wasn't her and she was gone. Nicholas thought he had been going crazy. Maybe, the last time in the park. The had looked into those eyes. The fear. The panic. She had run and he hadn't found her. Maybe that wasn't just a woman he had terrified. Could it be her? Did she want to be found? What happened to her?

"If she has been alive, shouldn't we ask ourselves why she had to fake her own death and why has she been in hiding all this time. She was an asset to her country. What would cause her to jump ship?" Brady suggested but the leader ignored her and simply switched onto the next slides. They showed images of Katy Jones meeting with Chinese war lords, Russian Mafia, Drug lords, senators, congressmen and several international diplomats. Always in the background just out of view but it was her.

"She has been working her way up to the highest part of senate. How she has gone untraced I would very much like to know." The leader said in an angry voice. Everyone in the room looked particularly baffled.

"This woman was skilled but she was never malicious. If she has been undercover for so long, we should be asking who is helping her. After all we didn't find out that agent Logan was dirty until it was too late." Brady pointed out and the room murmured in agreement. The leader looked like they could have steam coming out their ears.

"Are you suggesting that there is an enabler in our midst?" The leader asked which shut Brady up. Everyone else remained silent.

"How else would an amateur MI5 agent disappear right under the noses of the best intelligence agencies in the world," Nicholas pointed out, lounging in his chair next to Brady. The leader paused to mull over his point.

"Castle, you know how the target operates. You will be assigned to bringing her in. I want her alive. Don't let any personal feelings get in the way. Find out who is helping her or if she is acting alone. This is by order of the president. Do not let me down!" She warned and the meeting ended there. Nicholas got a lot of suspicious looks from his colleagues. He had to find Katy, not just for following his orders. He had to find out what had happened to his friend not just for himself but life had changed over the last couple of months.

"How?" Brady asked out loud. "How the hell did Alex get past all the security systems in the *world* and fake her own death?" Nicholas and Walter are sat in the room as she paced the floor. "You haven't had much to say on the matter?" Brady directed the comment at Walter as he typed a way on his laptop glancing up at Brady with a crooked grin.

"Well, while you have been yelling, I did a cross reference of the file pictures that we had on Alex and compared them to the scene pictures we had on her from the meeting today. Coupling that with the hacking equipment we gave her and the image dampeners. These emit minor untraceable signals when activated." Walter explained as his fingers flashed across his keyboard and he pushed his glasses further up his nose. Nicholas hid his smile from Brady.

"If they are untraceable then how are you tracking them?" Nicholas asked, sitting with his arms folded and only mildly paying attention to what Walter is doing next to him.

"You didn't let me finish. They are only untraceable to anyone but me. You do remember that the image dampeners were my invention." Walter explained, grinning at Brady who came round the desk to give her full attention to what Walter had. "Watch," He pushed the enter button on the keyboard. The screen illuminated with hundreds of markers across every continent but the map starts to home in over the USA.

"Blimey she's been getting around hasn't she," said Brady the dots intensify and Walter zooms in on the screen.

"She's been in Washington but the most recent location is just coming up." Walter explained as the beeping intensified and landed on New York. "The map said that she was in New York six hours ago." Walter announced triumphantly. Brady pulled out a radio and gets intelligence on the line. Using the coordinates, they got the area up on the screen.

"Why haven't you done that before?" asked Nicholas, raising an eyebrow at Walter. He smiled before explaining. Walter enjoyed telling people exactly how he got his results. Not for the glory of the attention but it was just satisfying to watch them sweat trying to keep up with him.

"Where was the need? I don't do random track and trace on everyone who uses my technology!" He exclaimed as Brady talked over the radio.

"There on fifth Avenue," Brady said and looked at the screen carefully. Nicholas examined the image carefully. "Wait, hold the footage." He said and Walter froze the screen. "That woman there," He pointed at the corner where a woman with heavy glasses was observing the camera with a smile. Walter zoomed in.

"Her face is different but there's something about that woman which is familiar. Brady is there any change of reversing what the image dampeners were hiding?" Nicholas asked. Brady looked at Walter questioningly instead of answering the question herself.

"Ahh once again let me work my magic." It took him a few minutes this time but as the screen refreshed and the image opened. There is an undoubtable proof that the woman in the image is Katy Jones. That was her coy smile when she knew something that you didn't.

"That's her!" Nick said aghast. It was like seeing a ghost. After all this time and all the months, he spent grieving. What happened to her? She was alive and well in the same city. Why didn't she reach out? Although that day at the café…

"Is there any way of tracing her from that point?" Brady asked, slapping Walter happily on the shoulder.

"Unfortunately, no, she turned them off and moved into unmonitored areas. She knows our blind spots. This was approximately six hours ago. She could be anywhere by now." Walter explained cracking his knuckles and starting to type furiously.

"Can you set up a scanner or an alert so if she turns them on again, we will know where to go and catch her." Brady asked sounding more excited by the minute.

"Already done, just linking it to your phones right now." Walter replied as his hands flew across the key board setting up codes.

"Wait do you think we can just show up and arrest her. Don't these work on the eyes as well. We don't know who is protecting her or what is her mission. She might abandon them all together and we will have no way of tracing her." Nicholas asked thoughtfully, they had to bring her in but how would they know what she was up to without further investigation. "What do you suggest instead?" asks Brady. Nicholas remained silent contemplating their options.

"Did either of you two ever hear the story of the enigma machine?" Walter asked and then continues when they both stares blankly at him in reply. "Alan Turing and a team who were tasked to break the Nazi code. They had thousands of different combinations possibilities which changed every day. yet they managed to break it. Did they go straight into battle using this information? No, they didn't. If they did then the Germans would have changed the whole system and they would have been back to square one all over again. They sat back, watch and observed and used statistics to win the war by making the most important moves against the Nazis without letting them know that they had broken the code. I suggest that we adopt a similar method here." Walter finished and Brady caught onto what he was suggesting. Nicholas takes a moment to catch up with the pair.

"So, you are suggesting if we watch and observe, see what her activities are and gather intelligence. We could not only find the perfect opportunity to bring her in but find out who she is working for and her motives?" Brady said snapping her fingers as the plan formulates herself.

"Precisely. Knowledge is power. We need to find a way of bringing her in quietly. Who knows what she is doing?" Walter finished with a sly smile on his face. He could be a massive nerd but he knew how to use it to win an argument or discussion.

"That sounds like a good plan. But let me just say that we should not underestimate this woman. She slipped through two secret intelligences lenses and for what reason. I never thought she would become the person she did when I was first assigned to her. Something isn't right and I can't put my finger on it." Nicholas contemplated aloud walking over to the window to look out on New York city. She was out there right now.

"What are you insinuating Castle?" Brady asked sounding hesitant already at his suggestion.

"Let me try to bring her in alone. I will use Walter's system. I know Alex. If I can get her to come to me and confide then maybe I can work out if she is a threat or not." Nicholas proposed but they both looked disbelieving.

"We are under orders of the president to bring her in. There is no higher power than that." Walter replied.

"I know, just give me some time. I know I can get through to her." Nicholas said with an air of desperation in his voice. Walter and Brady look at each other in despair. "Please for what we went through and what she did for our countries. We owe her a chance." Nicholas pleaded. Brady was tough but she had   a   soft   heart.

"Fine! I will give you two weeks, otherwise we do it my way." Brady replied as Walter rolled his eyes at her.

"Let's begin then." Walter in an exasperated voice and turned his attention back to the keyboard.

Nicholas chose to fail to mention that he had already thought he had seen Katy around the city before. There had been times he thought he was going mad, even chasing through the crowd and down side streets to find her. He thought that he was going mad.

Then one day he had been on a date, she was there in front of him. She fell. Right there at his feet and he helped her up. They made eye contact and she ran. He had nearly caught her but lost her in the crowd once more. Nicholas gave up after an hour of searching the park and alarming several runners. She needed help, if only she would show herself. If not, he'd have to catch her!

***

A week later, Nicholas was sat inside a bar looking out into the street. He had a hat and sunglasses on to cover his face. The image dampeners would have interfered with Walter's signal so he was doing this the old-fashioned way. He had a feed in his ear and surveillance on his phone.

"Ok keep an eye out," said Brady's voice through the ear piece. "Remember this is a track and observe. Don't get spotted."

"Yes, I know," Nicholas replied sarcastically into his coffee. It was probably the seventh time Brady had warned him. "Look out for a blue Audi R8," said Walter's voice down the com. Nicholas glanced at his phone and saw the tracker turn down the street and into his range of view. The car pulled up. The windows were blackened out but a man in a suit got out of the driver's seat and walked round to the passenger side to open the door. He couldn't see the man's face as it was obscured by a par of sunglasses. Probably some security detail Nicholas thought to himself. A woman got out of the passenger side and the pair embraced. She had long golden hair and her face was pretty but there was something not quite right.

"They're here." Nicholas said into the ear piece standing up to get a better look out of the window.

"Wait a second." Walter said, his fingers rattling on the keyboard as he coded, the face flickered on Nicholas's glasses and her real face was revealed. His heart skipped a beat. It was her. He took his glasses on and off. The difference was incredible. It was her laughing just like she had when she got out of the car before she died. He put his phone into his pocket and made his way out onto the road.

On the opposite side of the street, the driver went into the building while Alex took out her phone to answer a call. She looked apprehensive. There was a tap on the window from the first floor and she looked up to see the man waving down at her. Alex gave him a smile and a wave before her expression changing as she turned her attention back to the phone. Two different displays of behaviour. Who was she today; Alex, Katy or both? Maybe the man wasn't her body guard. Nicholas couldn't believe his eyes. How the hell did she survive? He snapped

"Castle, step down." Brady's voice urged as he left the café taking himself out into the open. He removed his sunglasses and walks across the street. He had to talk to her. His heart beat in chest. Alex had his back to him as she speaks angrily into the phone. With the glasses off he couldn't see past the dampeners but he didn't need them.

"Alex?" Nicholas blurted out as he worked up the confidence to talk to her. She turned round and looked at him. Even with the dampeners he can see that she was shocked. "Alexandra Shaw?" he asks again when she didn't reply. He eyes flashed with panic before her expression softened again.

"Oh no sorry, that's not my name." She smiled apologetically and turned away to her phone again.

"Alex I can see it's you." Nicholas said, resisting the urge to reach and touch her shoulder. "What the hell are you doing here?"

"I'm sorry but I'm not called Alex. You must be mistaking me for someone else." She said, her accent is more pronounced this time. She was speaking with a New York accent but the twinge of British was still underneath it. Nicholas took a step forward and put his hand on her shoulder causing her to freeze at his touch.

"What happened? I can help you? There's something I need to tell you." He said, looking into her eyes. Her expression changed from confused to annoyed. With a coy smile slipping onto her face, he knew that he was talking to Katy.

"I'm sorry," Katy replied with a delicate, dangerous softness in her voice. "For the sake of our old friendship I will let you go. Leave me alone." She warned, she reached a finger up to turn her dampener off for a second so that he can see her face. Nicholas gasped and smiled as the familiar features appear. It was his friend, nothing had changed. The relief he felt for her being alive consumed him that he did not notice the cars pulling up. Alex raised her hand and snaped her fingers.

Shite.

Crunch.

Nicholas woke up at the bottom of an alleyway in the dead of the night. Beaten and bruised. His equipment laying around him. The ear piece was still in. He groaned as he sat up feeling pain shooting through his ribs and a dull throbbing on the back of his head.

"Nice to hear from you again." Brady said down the coms. "Where are you, you have your tracker turned off." Nicholas looked round the alley as he listened to her scathing words in his ear.

"I don't know." Nicholas replied as he grabbed his phone. The screen had been smashed but it still turned on. He propped himself up against the wall as screen lit up.

"Got you, we're on our way." Walter said in a reassuring voice. Nicholas breathed in assessing what had happened. That was not the woman he once knew. What had happened to Alex? Had she become Katy? If so then God help anyone who got in her way.

Nicholas had to take a day to recover. The aching died down by the end of the day. The security had gone soft on him. According to the security cameras, Katy's thugs had knocked Nicholas out from behind and shoved him into the back of a van to be dumped in the middle of Harlem. Alex had gotten into a car and disappeared again. Her chauffer had disappeared and there was no trace of the man who had waved at her in the building. By the time they had issued a warrant to search the property nothing had been found.

"Your complete idiot," Brady said as Nicholas joined them in the forensics lab and took a seat at one of the computers. "You couldn't just leave her alone and follow instructions. Well guess what, she has abandoned the bio dampeners and Walter has lost track of her. There is nothing to follow. The dam woman has disappeared into the wind." She threw her radio across the room.

"I'm sorry, I had a lapse in judgement," exclaimed Nicholas, even though he was not guilty about his actions. "Something isn't right. We need to keep digging."

"How?" asked Walter sounding tired, he rubbed his eyes under his glasses staring at the screen. "We have no leads or way of bringing her in. We don't even know what she's doing or who's she's working for." He sounded pretty annoyed, even smacking the screen of the laptop as he spoke.

"What if I can get her to come to me?" asked Nicholas. Both of them stared at him with blank expressions so he continued. "I worked with her for years. I know how her mind works. There are certain things that she can't resist."

"After all this time what on earth would possibly possess fall for one of your schemes. She also worked with you. She would see it coming from a mile away?" Walter pointed out trying to shut down his idea. Nicholas glanced at him for a second. Walter was all for catching her but now he seemed a little reserved.

"I have two possible ideas. If one doesn't work then I can try the other more extreme idea." Nicholas explained without giving too much away. Something wasn't right. Walters eyes skipped between Nicholas and Brady.

"More extreme?" Brady asked. "Have you run this past HR at all?"

"No, you are just going to have to trust me." Nicholas replied in return. "You gave me a week. Let me try." Once again, Brady and Walter looked at each other despairingly.

"Fine but one more screw up and I swear you will be on desk duty for the rest of the year!" Brady warned him. That wasn't an empty threat. But then she would have to put up with him being in the office annoying her everyday so it was a loss for both of them.

"You don't even have the authority to order that." Walter pointed out her bluff and started laughing when she sent him a shut-up expression.

"One week." Brady said and points a finger threateningly at Nicholas. She left the lab in a huff and they could hear her swearing down the corridor.

"Way to go man, I've never seen her that pissed off." Walter seemed amused by the whole situation. "Anyway, what do you need?" Walter asked getting his fingers ready over the keyboard. This man created magic with his fingers.

"Nothing, I'm going to try this one myself." Nicholas said. This time he wasn't going to take any chances. He grabbed some pen and paper and set to work. Within an hour he had finished a fairly basic flyer and photocopied them for distribution. There was going to be no electronic trail with this plan.

Plan A for Atrocious

"An audition? Are you kidding?" asked Walter down the coms.

"I know it sounds crazy but believe me she will not be able to resist this." Nicholas replied. He had hired out the theatres on

42nd street. There was a lot of undercover agents in various roles and he had lined the streets with open audition flyers upon request. The production was for Phantom with open casting call for Christine. To his surprise nearly every woman under thirty in New York wanted to audition for the role.

"It's been four bloody days and there are civilians lining the street. How do you know which one is going to be Alex? She isn't using her image dampeners." A woman walked on stage and announced her name. There was no one else left for the day but this was a last minute auditionee. After four days Brady had called demanding what was costing the department nearly a hundred thousand dollars.

"Sorry were finished with auditions for the day." Nicholas said to the girl on the stage and held the phone away from his ear as Brady started shouting.

"I'm auditioning for the role of Christine." said a familiar voice from the stage ignoring his direction. The woman started singing and Nick looked round. Alex was stood in the centre of the stage smiling at Nicholas as she sang. He would have recognised her voice anywhere. Nicholas was in disguise so hopefully she wouldn't be suspicious.

"Brady, I'm going to have to call you back." Nicholas replied before she could belittle him anymore, cutting her off. She instantly tried to call him back. She was half way through the song as Nicholas put the phone into his pocket and listened to her sing. Did she recognise him? He failed to notice the theatre emptying around him until it was just the pair of them in the whole building. He had to let her finish. Once she hit the final note he whispered into his cuff. *Go.* Agents burst in at all sides.

"Katherine Jones, you are under arrest for fraud." One of the agents yelled dashing out onto the stage. Alex didn't move but simply smiled.

"Oh, am I?" she asked, she knew this was a trap. Nicholas stood up reaching for his gun. She looked at the agent.

"If you are even going to try to arrest me then you might as well get my name right!" She scorned him before turning her attention back to Nicholas. "Thanks for the chance to audition dear. *You know me so well.* But unfortunately, I know *you* as well." Katy finished and laughed. Nicholas vaulted over the rows of seats as Katy snapped her fingers. The trap door below her feet opened and she fell through away from the agents.

"Damn it, where is she?" Nicholas yelled. "I'm here," came a voice from behind them. "I'm here," came her voice from the box. "I'm here," Katy yelled from the side of the stage and disappeared with a burst of pyrotechnics. This caused momentarily blindness. The perfect opportunity to get away. The agents scattered to try and find her but Nicholas had failed. Trying to insnare her in a trap in her own world. She was teasing him by using different stunts the phantom used in the show. She had been a stage manager after all and she was making sure he knew that she had the upper hand.

"She's on the roof!" called a voice down the radio. Nicholas tore up the stairs. "She's locked the door," The report comes through the radio. Nicholas paused for a second and thought then an idea sprung to mind. He ran out into the foyer and found a window with access to the fire escape. He was able to squeeze through the tiny gap and reach the roof. Katy was standing there waiting for him. She held a gun ready.

"Not one step further *Nick!*" she ordered Nicholas but he moved closer with his hands up. She fired so close to his foot he flinched and got the message. "It's been lovely catching up but I'm afraid I've got to fly. Thanks for the laugh! *I really couldn't resist*" She called mockingly as a helicopter rumbled overhead.

A ladder fell out of the sky. She grabbed hold still keeping her eye on Nicholas and stepped on to the ladder.

"*Ta ta* dear friend. I hope our paths don't cross again. Make sure you do your homework next time!" She said as she was hoisted into the air and dumped the gun as the helicopter moved off. Katy could shoot. Why had she missed him? The ladder lifted her up into the air. Nicholas's ear piece went crazy. He ran forward and picked up the gun aiming it Alex's figure. She moved higher with each second but there was the shot. His finger trembled over the trigger. He breathed in but could not will himself to pull the trigger. And then she was gone. Nicholas yelled and threw the gun down. He couldn't do it. She knew him too well. He let out a scream of frustration as his ear piece rattled back into life.

"Brady wants to talk to you," said Walter's voice down the line. "Did you manage to get an ID on the chopper? I'm deploying a jet to follow them as I can't see it on the radar."

"Nope," Nicholas groaned waiting for the yelling to start. He walked over to the roof access door and allowed the rest of the team up.

"Castle, the gun, get it to forensics. We can scan it for prints or DNA," Walter suggested down the line. "How will that help?" Nicholas asked.

"Trust me, I need it." Walter said and then the line bleeped with another call coming through. Nicholas braced himself before answering.

"Castle what the actual hell was that?" Brady screamed at him. He pulled the ear piece out and threw it off the roof, shooting it out of the sky with perfect precision.

Plan B for barely even close

"So, you have no idea where she is?" Brady asked Walter again.

"I've got biometric scanners running on every continent. We have put out a warrant for her arrest. I have satellites scanning for her image dampeners. Air traffic control if constantly looking for the helicopter she took off in. No, I have not found her yet!" Walter replied irritably. Nicholas had dragged him into the dog house as their failed attempt to catch Katy.

"We need to approach this from a different angle." Nicholas said and pulled a white board up to work from. "What do we know about her so far?"

"Castle, I've said this once, I will not say this again. You are not on the logistics team." Brady berated him, the bags under her eyes making her look slightly mad. He was lucky he wasn't fired but Walter had convinced her otherwise.

"You know I can help." Nicholas said making a list anyway. "She's been seen around New York with that man."

"You mean her new body guard?" asked Walter looking up from his screen with a smirk on his face.

"We don't know that she could be playing him," Nicholas said and staring at his list, "The blue Audi, the helicopter. She came to the audition." He finished realising it was a very short list. "Walter, can you put up the distribution map of where she has been for me." Walters hands flew across the keyboard and a projector turned on showing a map of the world with dots all over Europe, northern Asia and across the US and the Caribbean.
"Well, that's so helpful," scoffed Brady but Nicholas ignored her.

"What do these places have in common?" he thought out loud looking at the map. "Why has she been in New York and Washington DC so much?"

"You said that the president himself wanted her followed right, why is that?" Walter asked.

"There was a threat detected to his internal affairs and issues instructions in the crime world to take her down without the press finding anything out. She has been linked to the conflict between China and Russia, considered a threat to the US. But as she was already dead, we ignored this detail until the recent DNA trace which was within the oval office itself." Brady explained revealing details they had not known before.

"How long has the bounty on been active," Nicholas asked scribbling on the board.

"There was one as soon as the Le Verne's were brought down but after her death the contract was complete. The estate she had managed was sent into a charity instead. The new bounty cropped up about six months later. Approximately three months after the president was inaugurated." Brady explained.

"What charity? I heard her money went into her sister and was confiscated by the Belize government." Nicholas asked.

"No, "Brady said, "It went into a foundation. It was called the Jones trust." Walter brought up the website. "This is a very small project. Surely with the estate that she left behind there would be a lot more expenditure."

"Unless the charity is just a front." Nicholas suggested. An idea popped into his head. "Walter, can you cross examine the dates and travels of the president with the locations and times of Katy's image dampener signal?" Walter set to work and three of them waited as the screen reloaded. The map lit up with green marks indicating matches for locations and times. The two coincided perfectly.

"Oh my god, she's following the president. She must have worked her way up high into the oval office itself." Brady said in disbelief staring at the map.

"Bring up a picture of all the female personnel for the president." Walter brings up a range of images. He flicked through them until Nicholas told him to stop seeing the face which covered Alex's with the image dampener.

"Jesus Christ. She is the president's media manager. Get the CIA on the phone." Brady said.

"Wait," Nicholas said. "Remember the enigma." This breakthrough was too important to tip her off that they knew. Katy was always one step ahead of them.

"I don't care. Harold, yes Miss Defraz. Arrest her right now." Brady ordered down the phone.

***

The interrogation light came on as the woman was cuffed to the desk. Brady leaned over her pressing the woman for any form of confession out of her. Katy must have spent a lot of time with her. This woman was the spitting image of Katy's disguise. Yet her hair was slightly different. It fell neatly around her shoulders rather than the crazy way Katy's did. Her mannerisms were different. Nicholas felt in his gut that something wasn't right.

"Katy. Turn the dampener off. We know it's you." Brady asked nicely but her patience was wearing thin after the hours of interrogation.

"I don't know what you are talking about?!" Miss Defraz cried out looking petrified. "I am a media logistics assistant to the president, nothing else!"

"Dam it," Brady slammed her hands on the table and walked out of the room and joined Nicholas in the adjoining room

"It's not her," Nicholas said quietly. Brady looked like she was at her wits end.

"How can it not be we have been following her for weeks. All the strings lead to this woman." Brady yelled as Nicholas continued to watch the woman in the interrogation room sob.

"Katy would keep up the act no matter what. She has been through a lot worse than this and is very well versed at being interrogated." Nicholas explained his thought process aloud. "She is also known for her reputation for getting away from being charged by intentionally knowing nothing about the crime," Brady pointed out. The door opened behind them and Walter walked in with a piece of paper and a grim look on his face.

"Walter, have you sorted out the image dampener. It is hidden in her skin?" Brady asked with a touch of urgency in her voice.

"No there was no trace of an image dampener." Walter said and pushed a piece of paper in Brady's hands. "Look at these DNA results. This woman is not related to Alex. We have her DNA and prints on record. They don't match. I think this is the real Miss Defraz."

"How the hell can that be?" Brady asks in a furious voice and grabs the piece of paper off Walter to have a look herself. "Why would Alex impersonate an innocent woman?"

"We've been led down a rabbit hole this whole time." Nicholas pointed out. "She knew that we were following her and sent us on a wild goose chase."

"Are you telling me that the FBI has been outsmarted by Alexandra Shaw?" asked Brady looking as though she could punch something.

"She couldn't do it on her own. Someone must be helping her. But why lead us here? What is she showing us with this trail?" He wondered out loud as Brady and Walter turned away ignoring him and started arguing. She had showed herself after all this time. Only let her presence be noticed now. Was it a plea for help?

No there was something else going on she was trying to show them. The dampener had shown them the traces of the presidents' journeys abroad. This woman was in charge of the logistics. She might be indirectly involved with some sort of plan from the man. We were investigating Katy on behalf of the president. Had she found something against him and gotten in too far and was no reaching out for help? Surely, she wasn't in this by herself?

"I say we approach this in two ways. Continue on like we believe this is the woman that we are after and investigate her work over the last two years. This woman is innocent but I think there is something really important linking her to Alex and it might be the only way that we are able to trace Miss Jones." Nicholas talked over Brady and Walters argument to get them to listen.

"You mean investigate the president himself? The man who assigned us to track and capture Alex in the first place?" asked Walter in an exasperated voice.

"That is exactly what I'm saying." Nicholas replies with half a smile. "She's leading us down a path, why not follow the bread crumbs and see where it leads. It's our only bringing her in."

"That is close to treason." Brady said sounding angrier than ever.

"Please let's just try this. We can find another way to bring Alex in. What would it help to get a little more information about what we are dealing with?" Nicholas asked. He wanted to believe his old friend hadn't turned into a criminal. "You know how smart she is. Let's follow her lead!"

"And what am I meant to report to the general. Oh, sir we are just investigating our own president to capture a woman he assigned to be brought in." Brady said mockingly.

"Think about it," Walter interjected. "Why are we investigating her? There has been no information or request even from above. There is no other evidence that what we have been told from the oval office. This is a direct order of the president. He knows of the Cover Girl. And…." Walter stopped mid thought as something clicked.

"No do you think?!" Nicholas asked as they both came to the same conclusion.

"What?" asked Brady.

"The president didn't hire her, did he?" Walter asked aloud.

"Think about it he was in his elections after Belize and her name was all over the dark web. Did he hire her for something to cover up what crime he committed and then she turned against him? Going against everything she stands for?" Nicholas thought out loud. They all stared at each other. The words sounded impossible yet they ringed truth. All three of them stared at each other in silence. What had Katy gotten herself into? Why did she suddenly need help?

Down the rabbit hole

Hello... it's me. Sorry I haven't spoken in a while, but I thought it was time to interrupt. The last time we spoke I had just been shot back in Paris. I went quiet. Sorry about that. There is a lot to tell you. God where should I start. Oh yeah, want to know what goes on behind the parliaments and presidential doors. Come with me, I will tell you everything I know...

Really this time I will but I'm going to do it in stages to make it a little more interesting. Sorry I know you wanted all the spoilers. Bit of an update. I no longer go by the name of Katy Jones or Alex Shaw. My name was compromised but the idea of the Cover Girl remained intact with my reputation; I am an idea, a service, a legend. Ok maybe not that last one but if you knew what I'd done then I might get a little more credit but I don't do this for the recognition.

I have gone by a new name over the last few months. I came up with this herself; Alex. I know right sounds dope AF. You can still call me Alex though. I have been working for a secret source infiltrating the presidential system. I can't tell you more than that but once again I got in two deep and this time there was no way out. For my own personal protection and my friends, I disappeared but the president has harnessed the full countries power to bring me in and if I do then a lot of people will be in danger.

I can't tell you why or there would be no point in all of this suspense. I haven't been working on my own but it's now gotten out of hand. Even for me, hard as it may be to believe. So, I have reached out for help from the best and brightest I know. After the last chapter I may have overestimated Nicholas's problem-solving skills. That ludicrous audition plan was just for fun to get them to hurry up and look at the bread crumbs I had left out for them to find. I couldn't make it more obvious. Do you think I really left my dampeners on open to tracing or did all of that mediocre work? You must be asking why Nicholas, Walter and Brady. Why ask for help when you have avoided them for so long? The risk was too high. This mission is too important. I get instructions down a secret channel and my techie helps me on the gadget side. Thanks to the investigations, I can't use my image dampeners as a disguise anymore so it's now onto wigs and latex.

Can you say that I have been skipping over asking what actually happened to me and why I had to fake my death. I will tell you that later but here is a summary. The truth is I had a message from someone very powerful asking for help. In return they informed me of the threat on my life. The person advised me to use it to disappear with a cadaver that looked like me to be left in the building in my place. I left everything there; my life, my friends and my freedom. I took on the new identity and move out to New York so that I could start my mission.

I was very clever with my finances. My ex-lawyer who still deals with my paper work took on the role of organising the charity but all the funds bar ten percent go into my bitcoin account which I use to get around and survive. Fair to say that the drug money is pretty substantial so that I was able to easily get set up in New York with an apartment in the upper west side and then one in Washington DC. That's where I am going to take you too now. Before we go on with the next part of the story, I need to tell you about my life after London and how the Cover Girl stepped up her game. For now, it was a matter of life and death...

Alex walked out of the phone shop. She didn't have much with her except one hand bag and a rucksack. The bio dampeners buzzed on her neck, projecting an appearance on to her face so that she wouldn't draw attention. Her hair was crazy as not having styled it in weeks it had reverted back to its natural state. *Soo much frizz.* She went to a Starbucks to set up her new phone. This was the start of her new life. No more hiding out in a safe house with endless deliveries and Netflix. *Looking back now it wasn't so bad.* After putting in all her details she had a depressing epiphany; Alex couldn't put any of her old numbers in. She skimmed through her new email account. The first payment had been made into her new bank account. Time to go flat hunting.

Alex called an uber which took her up to the flat viewings on fifth avenue. There was a large building overlooking the park close to where Rainier had stayed. *Are you guessing where I got the inspiration?* It seemed a waste of time to buy a place. If she paid in cash to my land lord who lived in the building then they will let her have this high rise, four bedrooms flat with no questions asked. She paid six months up front with a generous deposit. *The poor landlord would need it!* The place was kitted out to with every new device imaginable and a strong security system. The last tenant had been a *little* bit paranoid.

The place was huge. Alex sat down on the sofa and stare out on to the serein view of the park and the sky line behind it. It was very quiet up here. She waited for sunset before she got out the encrypted iPad. As soon as she was active a voice call came down the line.

"Hey," she answered, putting the iPad on speaker and sitting back on the corner sofa.

"Hello agent," replied the voice down the line in a sarcastic tone.

"Are you really going to talk like that?" She asked, looking into the camera where they were watching.

"No, it's just the way I have to address you now that you have taken on this task, plus this might be bugged. I need to make your new ID and passport but you need to decide a name." The agent said softening their tone.

"I was thinking Alex sounded pretty bad ass." Alex replied with a smile even though she knew they could see her.

"Where the hell did you get that from?" The agent asked but she could hear them typing.

"I thought of it herself." She lied.

"Really?" Came the agent's voice. She raised her eyebrow at the camera.

"Yes! No, I was thinking about Rainer's daughter and there was an actress called Alex in that new film that I saw on the flight over." Alex was cut off by the person groaning on the other line.

"God, you sound just like Nick." Alex thought and the image of him searching for her in the rubble came to mind and she went silent for a moment. "How is he?" she asked.

"You know that I can't tell you. You need to focus on the mission. You know how important it is!" They said remarkably softly, she felt a sense of pity in their tone making her heart sink a little.

"I know it's just a lot to adjust too." Alex said hugging her knees and fighting back tears.

"You can do it. You've got this. Now I have some instructions for you...

An hour later I hang up from the pre-recorded instructions with the boss. The moon was rising over the city so Alex decided to go out onto the terrace with a very large glass of red wine. The breeze whipped up over the side of the building blowing her untamed hair out of her face. The city stretched out in all its splendour. But it wasn't London. She had made the choice. She couldn't let herself get home sick. The work began tomorrow. She finished the glass and then head back into the flat to go to bed.

***

The dampers were fully charged so Alex placed them on her neck and felt the hum as they powered up. The image in the mirror was a pretty face with make-up already done. This was something that she had requested to save some time in the mornings. She pulled her wayward hair up into a hair net and place a blonde wig over the top. Even in the mirror the dampeners work. One final touch; the chip disguised over her throat which will change the vibration of her voice box programmed to give Alex an effortless New York accent. She tried it out and say as many cliched expressions as she could think of. The WIFI was not working in the flat yet but the iPad was 4G enabled but it couldn't leave the flat so she headed to Starbucks in search of data.

The nearest Starbucks happened to be right on the corner of the block and another one within five hundred yards further down the avenue. *Typical New York.* Alex sat outside with a frappa, mocha lappa, hatta dafuqachino. She loved watching the new world passing her by; the joggers, the nannies, the rich people driving past, the odd normal person in this neighbourhood. They don't give Alex a second glance.

An email pinged through from the interview at the senator's office. Alex got the job as a media assistant starting that very morning, not leaving much time to get over the jetlag. She picked up her horrendous coffee to start walking towards the nearest tube station. It made sense to try the route to work instead of trying to work it out during rush hour later in the day. Alex was so engrossed in the maps on her phone that she bumped into a man going in the opposite direction; knocking herself to the ground, flinging out her hands to catch her. Her coffee splashed over her but the new phone landed face down smashing the screen.

"Hey watch where you are going," Alex grumbled at the man irritably, whipping the spilt coffee off her coat. It was going leave a stain. The man grabbed her elbow to help her up looking very apologetic.

"I'm so sorry." He said, juggling the files in his hands to try and get an arm underneath her elbow. She got to her feet, as the man bent down to pick up the smashed phone.

"Oh great." Alex exclaimed and took her phone off him. The screen flickered bright green and then died. "Shite."

"I'm so sorry." He said again. "Let me buy you a replacement." The man offered as Alex glowered at him taking in his appearance. He was wearing a uniform covered by a large coat so she could not make out the badge. Someone to buy her a replacement would suggest that he had rather a lot of money.

"No, it's fine I just needed to get to work. It's my first day." Alex said through gritted teeth and contemplate how to get to work. She tried to shake the phone back to life. She knew the address; she just wasn't sure how to get there. Her mind jumped to the iPad upstairs yet it was too risky to use it out in public.

"Here, take this." He offered pulling out a check book. Alex blinked never having been given a check since she was maybe seven. This was probably an American thing. *More money than sense it would seem.* She declined turning on the charm to try to get away firm.

"No really thank you, I have to go. Can you just tell me how to get to Union Square?" She asked instead glancing at her watch.

"Let me do one better and have my driver take you." He offered instead. Alex blinked in surprise.

"That's lovely but then I wouldn't know how to get back." Alex answered trying to think about the subway map. Maybe she could ask someone who worked at the station.

"He will bring you back after you have finished." The man offered. He got his phone out and texted before she could say anything to stop him.

"I'm going to work for the whole day. He can't wait that long," Alex emphasised to try to change his mind, within thirty seconds a black saloon car pulled up right next to them.

"That's his job. He will have a new phone waiting for you on the ride home? Please accept my sincerest apologies Miss..." he paused as the driver got out and opened the door.

"Shaw," She replied dumbfounded.

"Well Miss Shaw, I wish you a good day and my apologies once again." And with that he walked off as the driver waited for Alex to get in. She accepted the door and slid into the leather seats which smelt pristine. It was about a twenty-minute drive. The car is a Rolls Royce Phantom; who needed one of these in New York? But it was a nice car. Alex mentally put it on her bucket list for after the mission.

The driver pulled up at union square letting Alex run to the senator's office. She glanced back to see if the car was going to drive off but it didn't. She shoved the ruined phone deep into her bag and hurried in. Her very first day and she was half an hour late. The receptionist was doing her nails and didn't look up as Alex ran to her desk.

"Hey is this senator Smith's office?" She asked and pulled out the piece of paper out of her bag. "I'm looking for Danielle."

The woman examined her nails while pointed her nail file at the door in reply. "Thanks." Alex said rolling her eyes as she followed the unenthusiastic directions. Time to start work as one of the senator's media assistants. The dampers vibrated gently on her neck reassuringly.

Safe to say the excitement didn't last. I am not built for menial labour.

A New Sensation; Tiredness

Six months later

Alex got in from the campaign office party with streamers stuck in her wig. The last six months had dragged by. She had never worked so hard in her life? How do people do it? The campaign had been successful and last night senator Smith got voted in as the senator representing New York at the white house in Washington. She pulled the dampeners off, released the voice clip and pull the wig off to allow her sweaty hair out of its itch fest. Her scalp sighed in relief. Her hair was so long now that she could barely get it underneath her wig.

The party was wild but Alex had to get back in order to receive instructions from the boss. The iPad started ringing as soon as she turned it on. She saw her tech guy on the line. She swiped up to answer and propped the iPad up on the table so they could see her. *I don't think in my whole like I had ever been so dishevelled and …. dirty.*

"Rough night?"

"Rough life, I don't think I'm cut out for the working world. I've been stapling and making coffee for six months. I'm going insane. Why am I doing this?" Alex groaned and slid onto the floor. Her ears were ringing still from the loud music

"You know why, we need to ensure that your identity isn't at risk."

"It was a rhetorical question!" Alex interrupted them.

"If the Cover Girl crops up too soon then the suspicions would be raised. I've started a buzz that there is someone taking over the role. The Cover Girl is still a phenomenon which the underground criminal crowds talk about," continued the tech guy without noticing her sarcasm. He shared a bunch of shared articles about her work which had been circulating.

"How do you know this." Alex asked looking through some of them.

"I have a mixed social circle." He replied matter of factly.

"From your basement?" Alex snorted in derision.

"Shut up, time to move on to the next phase of the plan."

"Finally, what do you need me to do."

"We need to you to set up the senator."

Alex blinked.

"What?"

"You heard me, you need to get the senator as a suspect for fraud or a conspiracy in the newspaper for something heinous. Then only the Cover Girl can get him out of it. Do you have any dirt on him?" he asked down the phone

"Of course, I do. I found out all the dirt within my first week. But it's more like he treats on his wife not illegal gambling or stock and bond scams." Alex explained, with all her hacking capabilities she had managed to infiltrate the senator's affairs from home to get everything she needs and the other assistants liked to gossip about their awful boss.

"Then you will need to plant some evidence, I will send the feds and get him investigated. This has to happen before you move to Washington." He said giving Alex a moment to make a mental calculation.

"That's in a week, how the hell am I meant to that?" She asked annoyed. The exhaustion was catching up with her. This on top of her work load would mean more nights of no sleep.

"Get creative *Katy,* we all know what you are capable of."

"Wait you are giving me free reign. You know this could get messy." Katy took over, rolling on to her chest staring at the iPad.

"I trust you, remember it has to be big." He reminded her.

"Oh, I can do big." Katy let out a sly chuckle as all the evil thoughts came to mind. Everything she had thought about doing while being subjected to the labour. *To be fair, I let Alex deal with that side of the mission.*

"I am going to regret this aren't I." said the Agent with a hint of apprehension. "It's been a while since you have let Katy loose." Alex had been moaning to him about how much of an ass hole the senator was for months.

"You said it not me." Katy gave a coy smile as she turned off the iPad. All the possibilities flew through her mind; she could create the biggest scandal that had ever been in New York. The excitement waned and tiredness crept in. This is too much thinking. She fell asleep with the iPad resting on her chest.

The phone vibrated loudly on the coffee table. Alex groaned as it buzzed again sending ripples right through her. She flapped her hand on the table but the phone was out of reach. It was moving across the table away from her with each rattle on the metal. She stretched further and rolled right off the sofa to land face first on the hard wood floor. She swore loudly as she finally got the phone and pressed it to her ear without looking at the number.

"WHAT?"

"Alex. You are late," said the voice of the senator.

"Shite shite SHITE!" She exclaimed and checked the phone clock which read eleven thirty.

"Have you got a cold; your voice sounds different?" The senators voice asked impatiently; she didn't have her voice chip on. Smacking her hand against her face she put on the worst accent and muffled the microphone.

"*I'll be right in,*" She replied hanging up and diving into the bedroom and pulling out something fresh to wear. After a ten second turn around, she pulled her wig on haphazardly, place the voice chip on her neck and placed the dampeners under her ears. They came to life as the lift door opens and Alex saw her appearance change in the reflection of the doors. She ran out into the foyer, through the doors and onto the street. The only way to get to the office was to hail a cab. It was hard to be seen amongst the throng of people. Then out of the corner of her eye; she saw him…

Nicholas was walking down the opposite side of the street. Could it really be him? A taxi pulled up next to Alex but she was too stunned to hear the driver who yelled at her. Without a moment's hesitation, she crossed the street and followed him from a distance. She recognised where he was going. The café they met when she was hiding. Before everything changed.

Alex sat down a couple of seats away looking right at him. His gaze flickered over her but he didn't seem to register that there was anyone else in the world. He looked strong yet sad. She wondered how the last few months have been for him. Awful she guessed and it was all of her own doing. She felt a twinge of guilt in her stomach and it took all of her strength not to approach him.

Nicholas took out a pen and paper to write something down. He was so engrained in his work. It took him some time as he ate pancakes while he finished. She could see a glint of a tear in his eye. Alex's phone buzzed again but she chose to ignore it. Her eyes fixed on Nicholas as he finished up and puts his writing into an envelope leaving it on the table. Nicholas's phone started to ring as he got up. He sighed like a weight has been lifted off his mind before answering. Alex couldn't stop herself; he was five paces away when she got up and swiped the envelope off the table, hurrying across the street. Nicholas paused and returned to leave a tip. She hid at the entrance to an alley way as he looked up and down the road.

Nicholas looked over as the waitress pointed in her direction hid herself and waited for him to leave. She crouched behind a dumpster as she opened the letter. It was addressed to Alex not Katy.

I won't tell you what he wrote but it pulled at even my soulless heart strings because he was saying goodbye and moving on with his life. It wasn't written to me after all yet we are one and the same. The words were so touching but I realised he was also letting go of the idea that I was ever going to talk to him again. He was going to move on with his life and I had to move on with mine. The glimpse of the life I left behind left me sad but I had to focus on the task in hand. I was going to commit to this and have to get serious.

Alex went home before heading to the office. It was nearly lunch time when she arrived looking fierce AF. She was full with a new found confidence and inspiration until she saw the senator standing right by her desk. *Shite.* She walked past him without making eye contact and booted up the computer.

"Miss Shaw, I am aware that we all celebrated our victory last night but I expect all my staff to be here on time. Not four hours late." He asked in a condescending tone. This was the first time he had acknowledged her existence.

"Well, I was doing extra research before I came in today." Alex lied looking him directly in the eye.

"What on?" He asked sharply, his hands migrating to his hips.

"Erm, Washington fashion week?" She guessed and Senator Smith started laughing, dropping the strict persona.
"I hope that this will not happen again. There was something that I wanted to tell you. I have seen the hard work that you have been doing around the office and I think it is time for you to be promoted. As my personal assistant. How does that sound?" He asked, smiling with a hint of crazy in his eyes. Alex smiled on the exterior but inside she was dying at the thought of having more responsibility.

"Me what happened to Randy?" Alex asked looking round the office to see that he wasn't there.

"Randy has been caught feeding information to the opposition so I fired him for gross misconduct." The senator replied, still looking enthusiastic

"That's awful." She replied trying to keep a straight face. *If he only knew.*

"I need people on my team who I can trust." Smith said looking at her scathingly. *The irony, he didn't have a good judge of characters from the offset.* Though as his assistant it would put Alex in a better place to set him up. She smiled and accepted the position gracefully finally getting her to leave her desk to contemplate her plan.

The next few days pass by and Alex struggled to come up with an idea. Time was ticking. He had whipped the system and she couldn't find the illegal bonds. She even tried flirting with him.

She might as well have flirted with a snail. How was she going to take him down?

Washington DC

They moved the office to Washington for a few days and Alex was at his side day and night. She wasn't used to this lifestyle and the tiny flat she had to share while they were there. This promotion was not her cup of tea. Alex barely had space to breathe let alone move. There was no occasion where she could consult the tech guy as there was zero privacy so it remained in her bag. Her phone was constantly buzzing with the senator's emails. The pay rise was an actual joke. Thank God she still had Katy's income to look after herself. *This was torturous.*

On the last day in Washington, she saw her opportunity. Another senator was trying to push the most disgusting bill. The act of making abortion illegal apart from in risk of life of the mother. Senator Smith would never advocate the bill but if it got out in public that he had raised support for it then there would be public outcry. Alex decided to work late one night waiting for everyone else to go home. She disabled the cameras using a video loop, replaced her wig and set the image dampeners to a new setting. The new dampeners had an upgrade which can scan and mirror someone's image. She took the image of a woman she saw assisting the president himself. Alex created pledge a letter of support of the senator pushing the bill. Not only that she started a trail so scandalous that Senator Smith would be lucky if he stayed in office. Looking back, she might have gone a little too far. She alerted the press and send copies of the sensitive documents before forging his signature. Even leaving his finger prints over the documents with gloves she had made with his fingerprints. Tomorrow, Alex would get the senator out of the predicament.

After barely any sleep Alex bounced out of bed to prepare herself for the day. *Pay back deserves a fancy outfit.* She had some new equipment delivered from the iPad. For the first time in months, she went outside without her bio dampeners on. Alex programmed the security to see a loop of her working in her office while she could go out. *Was I worried about being recognised? Not here. No one was looking for me and I wanted to be completely authentic. There were not many cameras on my route which I used a hat to obscure my face.* The press was gathered outside of the steps of congress as the new bill was announced. The supporters and protesters lined the streets ready to make their voices heard.

It was extremely entertaining standing in the crowd with her hair down and sunglasses on just in case. The senator's names were called out and a lot of them were standing their ground. The evidence she had planted set the crowd into a rage and the senators were utterly confused. Laughing Alex headed back to the flat to get ready and go back into the office. She put the dampers on reluctantly. What a short thrill to be herself just for a few hours but the excitement was over for now. She sighed as she left the tiny apartment.

***

"Alex, where have you been? asked Senator Smith as she entered the office. *Maybe the loop hadn't worked.*

"Sorry, just getting my bearings." She replied settling herself at her desk, hiding her smile from him.

"I know there is a lot of history here but visit it on your own time OK!" Senator Smith scolded Alex and went into his office swearing. The pressure had gotten too him, his friendly fake persona falling away to show the real side of him. *A p***k.*

"He's in a good mood," Alex pointed out sarcastically, taking a seat and powering up my computer. Sometimes her British sarcasm seeped through before she could stop herself.

"I think he's just stressed about the abortion mandate discussion this afternoon. Leave him be." Janice, senator Smith second assistant implored Alex. "He doesn't need wayward employees being mediocre at their jobs today." Janice added her scathing comment. She looked more stressed than the senator did. She was a massive suck up. Janice would have ratted Alex out to the senator the day that she slept in.

"Get your head out of his ass, the air is much fresher." Katy retort as she accessed her files. The other office employees snorted as Janice looks affronted. *Sorry, I couldn't help myself.*

An hour passed before they had to go into the congress where the discussion of the abortion bill takes place. Alex watched in the stands with the other staff as the senator's pledge allegiance and the session begins. The bill is announced and broadcast live on television the names of sworn support were read out. There are about two dozen and sandwiched in the middle is read Senator Smith of New York.

Alex looked aghast as the other office workers exchanged worried glances. The icing on the cake was seeing Senator Smith melting down in his office. The damage was done. The names were released to the public before the session ended and the media uproar started within minutes; naming and shaming articles, tweets, hate mail, death threats from woman's right campaigners. Alex could see the social media notifications coming in. *I sent a few of the clever tweets.* Smith called an emergency meeting in five minutes. Everyone ran around like headless chickens while Alex tapped on the iPad to the boss.

"I can't wait to see how you get him out of that one. □□□" The text read from the boss. She smiled and head into the office for damage control. It might be a challenge but she knew what to do. This weekend Katy Jones is coming out of retirement.

FINALLY!! I'm free!

Old Habits Die Hard

Katy walked into the small, classy bar in a skin tight dress, red bottom heels and faux fur coat. She ordered a dirty martini while she waited at the bar. This was more of a speak easy that an actual bar and very secret. Some celebrities were enjoying time in private canvased booths while waiters discreetly took their orders. This was the place that you know you will not be disturbed. Katy was approached by a few men at the bar but she sent them on their way.

Tonight, Katy had let her own hair down which had grown so much in the last six months after being hidden under a wig. No damage or heat meant it shined in any light with a healthy glow, reaching her waist. It is also an effective shield to hide behind to do some distance observations. She wasn't completely free. The dampeners hummed on her neck projecting a new face. *I may be Katy Jones again but I won't risk being recognised if word gets out there is a new Cover Girl in business, then it would be a disaster. What a thrilling night.*

Senator Smith walked into the bar and looked around. He seems more tired than usual. The press and public have been hounding him for an explanation for his secret support of the abortion criminalisation bill which had grown in strength after being shown such outright support. Politicians really are mindless sheep! The senator comes over to Katy and sat down.

"Excuse me? Is you name-"

"Jones, Katy Jones."

"Ahh Miss Jones, I have been recommended you down the grape vine. Is there somewhere we can go to talk?" Katy snapped her fingers and the barman showed them over to the most private booth in the room; the champagne was waiting on ice. Katy opened it up and poured it herself setting the precedent that she was leading the evening. The tab was going on his bill so she didn't' feel guilty getting the most expensive one. An assistant's wage doesn't go very far and Katy believed proper champagne was a necessity. *After putting poor Alex through the ringer for all this time, he owed her some sort of repayment.*

"I am in dire need of your service. I have been framed and it is threatening my position in office."

"I'm aware of your situation Mr Smith. I did read all one hundred and twelve very detailed emails you sent me."

"Ahh yes I'm sorry. I have been most anxious to get this matter dealt with and I am afraid I don't know who I can trust."

"That is exactly the way you should be thinking."

"Can I trust you?"

"No, but I am the only person who can help you."

"What is your fee?"

"Ten down, then another ten after I have completed the contract plus expenses." Katy replied with a coy smile. It's helpful to know how much the client makes and she had personal access to all his accounts. *Even the hidden ones.* This is a bit steep but it will give her the cash flow.

"Fine, I have cash here." He handed it below the table. She took the cash and quickly rifled through it to count and then tucked it in the garter under her skirt.

"I also need your assurance that we never met. You do not speak my name or share any image of my face." Katy stated before she left. No paper trail gave her no legal protection and no personal protection meant that she was vulnerable. Though the tech guy was listening in through the dampeners. He had added bugging equipment and GPS tracking.

"You have my word." Smith replied and Katy left the bar through the back entrance. *God if men know their place it's so much easier to negotiate.* She pulled her coat inside out, tucked her hair up into a hat from her pocket. Then refreshed the image dampeners before emerging out of the alley. Job done and Alex flagged down a taxi back home. She took the long way. *Cheers to a job well done and quickly.*

When Alex got into her flat, she collapsed onto the sofa exhausted from the excitement and workload. She pulled off her layers, shoes, dampeners and make up. Being Katy was so much easier when she had close security protection however that wasn't an option anymore. Never again was Alex going to put her trust in anyone over her own life. To say that she had trust issues was an understatement even though Nicholas was a dear friend.

The iPad rang and she picked it up slumping on the cushions. Alex pressed the remote for the blinds to go down and the fire to start. To her surprise it wasn't the boss it was her tech guy. She rested her eyes while he talked

"Evening Jones."

"Hush you, Shaw here."

"I take it he took the bait?"

"Yup, it's your turn now." Alex said pulling out the wad of cash that was half of her years' salary and placing it on the table

"Already taken care off. Come the morning there is going to be headlines of a forgery on the official documents. The incriminating evidence is lined up and the bill leader will be arrested tomorrow for terms of fraud and breaking the constitution. That ridiculous bill will be thrown out for good." He sounded jubilant over the line.

"Excellent. Thankyou. I could have done that but with work and everything the effort would have balled me over." Alex said, inspecting her nails. No way on earth would she have done that. The footage of her forging the documents in the federal office would be released but too distorted to get any features to lead it back to Alex.

"True but now comes the hard part; you have to find a way to get in with the president, leaving a bread crumb trail for him to find later. Only you don't work in his department. Working for him yourself is too risky so we need to find another way." The tech guy mused over the call. Alex heard a tone in his voice that was unsettling.

"It sounds like you are doubting me?" Alex replied looking at the camera.

"This is a complicated set up with a high level of risk. There is no space for mistakes. Our commander needs this to be executed precisely. He knows the ins and outs of every inch of that office."

"Yes, I know. It will be done." Alex said and hung up without saying goodbye. Having as techie on her side was helpful but as always, she didn't like leaving her fate in someone else's hands.

What other choice did she have? With no room for error and the commander depending on this plan there was nothing else to do but put her trust in these people. At least they were at arm's length and not in her home. Even though Alex's body was tired, her brain was buzzing from the stress. She tried walking out on the balcony and doing some light stretching. The weather was getting stuffier as summer drew in but the nights still had a little bit of a chill.

Alex let her hair blow free in the wind. The thought of her hair under a wig in the hot weather made her scalp itch. A run would calm her nerves. Going back inside she turned on the treadmill. Nothing happened so she tried hitting it instead. The thing was broken. After emerging as Katy this was a risk but she needed to burn off this nervous energy.

She put on her running shoes, put the dampeners back on and head out of her apartment with her natural hair up in a pony tail. Being on the upper west side central park is literally on her door step. Within a few minutes she was at the mile-long lake. It was late yet people were still out jogging in the safety of the streetlights. The music pounded in her ears making Alex just let everything disappear in to the beat of the bass and her feet pounding on the concrete.

The light gradually changed from the glow orange and the night sky appeared. This was the only spot in the city you could see the stars. Alex veered off from the lake and cut through the park towards the boat house and the famous bridge. There were normally tourists here taking pictures of the famous filming locations and the occasional horse and carriage so she didn't feel nervous. Tonight, the part was particularly quiet. She kept her mind clear and turned a corner to loop round back towards the street. But the path was particularly dark with the shadows of the trees obscuring the lights. She jogged right into a hooded stranger

She stumbled back apologised but the stranger didn't reply. They grabbed her by the arm to stop her falling over. Their grip tightened as she got her balance and looked up at him to see his face covered. Alex grabbed her phone and handed it over hoping that was all he wanted. The man took the phone and threw it into the bushes. *Crap!* Was he alone? Alex warned him to get off her. He didn't release his grip, not saying anything. With one fluid movement she pulled his arm back and flipped him to the ground rolling herself on top of him. He was pinned.

Another two figures appeared out of nowhere and blocking her escape. One of them was a foot taller and built like a house. Alex tried to bring him down but there was nothing she could do. He knocked her round the head and pulled her into the bushes out of sight of the path, pinning her down. Alex kept her mind clear. She used her legs to push the man away trying to think of the next move to get him off her.

The old flashbacks started; she hadn't suffered from them in so long. She cleared her mind to consider her options. Her tech guy had her tracking but he didn't know she had gone out. With her arms and legs restrained all she had was her voice. Alex yelled as loudly as she could and her voice echoed through the silent night. The brute covered her mouthed but Alex bit him to get him to let go. He grabbed her head and smacked it off the ground.

That hurt! It was the motivation she needed. This guy was going to suffer!

 The adrenaline pulsed through her, as her eyes watered. This is not going to happen to her again. Alex got one of her legs free and booted one of the men in the face as there was a rustling in the bushes.

Out of nowhere a massive dog charged at the men; teeth bared, barking ferociously. One of the men backed off as another dog appeared. The dog was as white as snow with saliva hanging from its mouth as it snarled. I call out again and the dog barked. Another dog, an Alsatian appeared at the white one's side. It was enough to scare Alex too.

The men released her to swat at the dogs; they both sprang at one each, deep growls rippling from their throats. Alex heard the crunch as the white dog broke the man's forearm as he howled in pain. He tried to get the dog off him but it anchored itself down and pulled him to the floor. The Alsatian bit the brute of men but he was pounding on the dog's head to make it let go. The last man pulled Alex up and used her as a shield as the massive white dog released his friend and snarled with blood around its muzzle. Her heart lifted as she heard voices and sirens. Alex called out as the white dog lunged at both of them and its teeth connect with the man's ankle. He winces and lets her go. She caught herself on the rocks as the dog attacked the man right next to her face. She didn't dare move.

Alex heard a determined shout and the white dog lets go of the man who ran into the bushes and out of sight. The white dog then turned on the remaining attacker; the red blood staining his white fur. The Alsatian had done some of damage yet the man was still holding his ground. He still wanted to fight as both dogs snarled at him with their hackles raised. Alex pushed herself onto her elbows and tried to ease away as they attacked again.

Suddenly the sound of sirens and yells came from the path. The cops finally found them, taking control of the man off the dog as the Alsatian continued to bark at him. The large white dog turned towards her. The blood drooling out of his mouth as it padded nearer, hackles still raised.

Alex froze and avoided direct eye contact. The dog sniffed her face, gave her a lick slavering with the attacker's blood and then proceeds to lie on top of her. His weight over Alex's legs stopped her from getting up but his presence was comforting as the cops deal with the attackers. The Alsatian was called off and the handler approached her. She heard a low grumble in the dog's stomach which rippled through his chest.

"Archie it's ok, well done." The handler said. The white dog laic his head on the ground and whined. The Alsatian bounced over to sniff Alex too. The handler looked oddly familiar. The Alsatian was a completely different dog; playful and happy. The officer hooked up the white dog to a leash causing him to get off Alex's legs.

 "Miss?" the handler asked Alex but her head was ringing from the blow to the back. Had he been speaking to her all this time? The dog nudged her in the ear as she made eye contact with him.

"What?" Alex asked confused.

"Can I help you up? Anything broken?" He asked and reached out a hand to her.

"No, I'm fine." Alex replied but when she realised her legs had turned to jelly as she took his hand and stood up. The Alsatian presses its body against her legs panting happily. It was a completely different dog.

"Let me help you over to a bench." The handler suggested and they walked back to the pathway where there was a bench under a lamp post. The three men are lying on the ground next to each other in the light being dealt with by the paramedics.

"She attacked us!" one of them cried out as she emerged.

"Yeah right!" replied one of the officers shutting them up. Alex felt shaky as she sat down. The white dog jumped up to lick her face again. It pulled her attention away from the assailants to the dog.

"Archie down." The handler said. She notices that he was not in uniform like the other policemen. Archie sagged onto his side and paws at her leg to get a stomach rub. If it weren't for all the blood, he would be an adorable mass of white hair. Alex willingly took the distraction. "I hope they didn't alarm you miss." The handler said while scratching Archies head as the other one looked up at us with a goofy expression.

"Where did they come from? How did they know what was happening?" Alex ruffling Archies ears. How was this the same dog that had torn a chunk out of that man's legs?

"We were walking in the park and they just took off. I volunteered to give them some extra exercise. I heard their warning barks and called for backup. It took me a couple of minutes to find you as I had to apprehended the third person. My colleagues were here within two minutes and Archie and Waffle were doing their jobs." The man explained. Alex looked at the man's face properly to smile and blinked as she recognised him.

"Didn't you lend me your car once?" She asked as she stopped patting Archie. He squirmed beneath her in protest.

"Yes," he said, thinking hard. "I broke your phone. Have you changed your hair?" He asked looking her up and down properly.

"Yes, I remember," Alex replied as the pair of dogs started bickering over her attention. Archie then pressed his paw on her torso which hurt pretty badly. The adrenaline was over so she really gasped at the pain. Waffle sensed it thinking Archie had hurt her. Alex flinched from the flying jaws as Waffle bared his teeth.

"Enough." The man said and the pair stopped and looked at them sitting quite innocently.

"Wow! They are really well trained, "Alex observed as the pain subsided but she edged away from them. Those teeth were as alarming at the attackers were.

"Some of the best in the service, please don't be alarmed. They are being extra protective over you. Waffles is young so Archie puts him in his place sometimes." The handler said curiously. He demonstrated as he reached a hand to her shoulder and both eyes lock on following his direction. Even Waffles heckles raise a little. One look from the handler and they both backed down.

"How do they know who to go after? Have they been trained to recognise victims?" Alex asked trying to distract herself trying to calm her nerves. The handler was all too keen to share his secrets.

"They have been trained in defence and submission of armed criminals. We train them from puppies in all sorts of scenarios. Normal police dogs go after someone directed by the handler. Theses ones have been taught basic techniques to protect victims including comfort and position hold. A little bit like service dogs," He continued. "Waffle is still young. But Archie will keep a victim still and provide a second protection to officers and victims in case an assailant escapes or the victim panics." He explained. "I don't handle them full time. I used to before I moved up the ranks. It's nice to help out now and then. They are on respite care with me at the moment." The handler was interrupted by a female officer.

"Is he talking about the dam dogs?" She asked in a think New York accent.

"It's not like they aren't the heroes of the night, were they?" The man replied with raised eye brows and she rolled her eyes in response but the pair smiled at each other.

"I need to take you to hospital and then the station for a statement." The officer explained gesturing towards the ambulance. Alex felt a fleeting moment of panic. The dampeners could be detected within police or federal offices seeing. She wouldn't be able to remain disguised.

"No, I would rather just go home." Alex said standing up too fast and swaying a little. "It's getting late. I don't have insurance. Can I just make a statement some other time?" She asked. This was a very common excuse as ambulances and hospital visits came with big bills.

"That's your choice but it is important to press charges to get these men off the streets in case they attack someone else." The officer replied but she still looked a little concerned.

"I know but I just feel a little over whelmed right now and the thought of going into a building and seeing them." Alex explained looking around for reasons to leave. She could feel bruises rising on her face and a cracked rib. Nothing serious. She could tell the officer was getting frustrated.

"How about I take her statement tomorrow?" asked the handler.

"Captain that is not your responsibility?" The officer interrupted. He shot her a look which even Alex knew meant back off and she put her hands up in the air and walked away. The scene cleared leaving just the pair of them and the two dogs in the park. He was a captain, high up in the force. This wasn't good.

"Let me help you home." The captain offered. "Take my arm it will make walking a little less painful, are you sure you don't want to go to hospital? You can use my insurance." Alex cut him off before he could say anything else. Why was a Captain showing her so much interest?

"No that would be fraudulent. I need to be at work tomorrow." She took a step and a pain shot up the side of her shin and he offered his arm. "How did you know my ankle hurts?" Alex asked taking his arm.

"Archie alerted me." The captain replied as Archie sniffed at her side.

"He's some dog," Alex replied admiring his light coat. He was a white Alsatian, nearly twice as big as Waffle. They started walking back towards her building. It took a while and she grew more nervous. Anyone we meet in the park see Archies blood-stained coat and give us a wide berth. They got to her building within fifteen minutes. She paused to thank him so that he wouldn't see her flat number. He might not believe she didn't have health insurance if he saw it. "I will come to your office tomorrow to get your official statement. Here is my card." The captain asked, it read: Captain James Hart of the NYPD.

"Sure," Alex replied and stowed the card in her pocket. "Though, I would assume that you would want a detective to handle the case." She asked nonchalantly.

"As it was the service dogs which helped you and I was responsible for them tonight. I want to ensure that nothing went wrong. It will be your word against the convicts." James informed her sounding official. "Stay safe," he asked and left the foyer. Alex turned to the lift but Archie was sat in front of her.

"Archie come." James called, Archie whined and pressed his head against me. "Now," James ordered more sharply. Archie whined as if to say sorry to leave you and trotted out the door into the night. Much like Ghost from game of thrones. Alex slumped against the lift doors as it rose up. She went straight to the bathroom to pull off the dampeners and check the damage. She could feel a bruise forming on her cheek. A good corker around the left eye and it was throbbing. The dampeners would need to be calibrated over night to hide the shadows. She put the dampener back on and noticed her face did not change. Had it not been working the whole night? Alex went into the lounge and picked up the iPad to call her tech guy.

"What?" He asked blearily. She had have woken him up.

"I've been seen by a police captain." Alex hissed in a mild panic.

"What?"

"I've been seen with my real face." She repeated in frustration.

"Can we dispose of him?"

"No, he's an important officer in the NYPD." Alex curled onto the sofa as the tech guy woke up properly. He thought for a moment before replying.

"Well, you know what they say, keep your friends close and your enemies closer."

"He's not my enemy," Alex rolled her eyes and fiddled with the dampener.

"Anyone who sees your face is. You are going to need to get close to him to make sure he doesn't work anything out. How did this happen anyway?" He asked.

"Well..."

****

The phone buzzed on the table making a horrible rattling sound jolting Alex awake. She reached for it as the noise coursed through her and slid off the edge of the sofa. It wasn't my alarm going off; it was a call from her office. She let the number ring out. The voice mail flashes and Alex pressed the button. It's Jenny from her office telling her to get down here with the senator's coffee the news storm was approaching. She groaned and pushed herself up to her feet. Alex took a step and swore as she felt the jab of pain in her ankle. She hobbled over the kitchen and noticed that there was a package waiting for her under the front door.

She found a new set of image dampeners inside. The note read that these are two-way systems. Everyone will see the disguise as before except for the police captain when it recognised his facial profile. It would refilter Alex's face to be normal so he wouldn't notice the difference. To everyone else it would be different; Alex was impressed with the techie but if she told him she would never hear the end of it. She was just going to have to keep the blonde wig and come up with an excuse in the meantime. Hair was easier to explain than why her facial features kept changing.

Alex jumped in the shower making herself look presentable before heading into the office. The bruise on the side of her face was pretty grim. Today she set the filter to look extra done up and confident. She put on a dark blue jumpsuit with a fitted waist and her new red bottom heels and head out to work.

The car pulled up outside the office at 11.30am and Alex snuck inside with her laptop bag and a tray of coffees. *Only three hours late.* The office was deserted office and to her horror she saw everyone in congregated in the meeting room for damage control.

"Glad to see that someone thinks she is good enough to join us?" said Senator Smith as Alex slide in. Everyone turned round to stare at her

"I'm sorry I was mugged last night." Alex tried to explain putting down the coffees and getting out her notebook.

"Well as my assistant media manager I thought you would be first here to handle damage control after the bill scandal." He nearly screamed at her. She looked at him confused. The board had the headline with the abortion bill being scrapped due to fraudulent signatures being added including Senator Smith who had been cleared of all allegations. He had made a huge donation to family planning and woman support. Now was the time to push his name forward. Alex took her bollocking with her head down making notes. *Lucky escape pr**k.*

The rest of the meeting continued on and everyone was sent to work with various roles. Alex was asked to stay behind by the senator. She couldn't afford to get fired and lose her access to the office in Washington. The Senator left the meeting room door open so that everyone could her. He took up his stance and she waited for him to explode.

"Do you want to be here?" He asked curtly.

"Yes of course." Alex replied before he cut her off again. *This guy has a superiority complex after being bailed out by a woman.*

"If you did then you might show up on time. I don't want this lame excuse of mugging for a reason for you to be late. I expect everyone to be here before me and leave after. This is your life. This job can make your career and it requires 100% of your dedication." He growled and eyeing her up and down.

"I expect someone or something has been distracting you from the expensive get up you have on today. How can you afford such shoes? Even I know I don't pay you enough. Been whoring yourself out and just using mugging as an excuse to cover your tracks?" The senator yelled losing his control. It was such a massive leap from being late to work to being accused of prostitution it took her a second to process the leap he made. *Oh, please let me at him!* Alex opened her mouth to react. *Supressing me! Stand up for yourself girl!* When someone coughed from the doorway.

"I can assure you Senator that her story is perfectly true."

Captain James stood in the door way looking magnificent in his uniform; sunglasses, hat and polished shoes smiling at her. Alex didn't need him to rescue her however, having an eye witness would be very helpful at that very moment. Her stomach gave a small flip at the sight of him. *What was that about Alex?*

"Senator if you require to see the report, I have a copy right here." Captain James addressed Smith.   The Senators whole demeanour changed; is public face and creepy smile emerging.

"Officer, I mean Captain Hart," Smith corrected himself, stumbling over his own words. "I was not aware we were due to come into the office. I assume you are here to look after my valuable employee here, Miss…" He stopped within his over eagerness forgetting her name on the spot. Alex resisted rolling her eyes as she watched him crash. James maintained his polite persona.

"Yes, sir I am here to take a statement from Miss Alex for her mugging last night. I thought she might like to share it with me over lunch as it was quite an ordeal last night. But I can tell that you are working hard so I do not wish to intervene on her duties" The Captain explained; Alex knew exactly what he was doing and kept her expression level.

"Yes, I was just discussing that with Miss Alex and assuring her that she can take *all the time off she needs to recover*. No problem." Senator Smith grimaced in her direction; he was red with anger and embarrassment. *This was just embarrassing. I love it!* The door was open so everyone could hear how full of shite he was.

"If you wouldn't mind, I would like to borrow her for a while so I can take her statement in private." Captain James asked and the senator nodded. Alex had no choice other than to gather up her bag and follow Captain James out of the meeting room. She motioned him toward her desk. James was already heading towards the exit. Alex followed him onto the street expecting to see a cop car to take her to the station but there was nothing waiting for them.

"Where are we going?" Alex asked, catching up with him in her heels, swinging her bag over her shoulder. She held in a hiss as it banged off her sore rib. He simply kept walking down the block and round a corner to a little restaurant tucked in between two shops with a great view of the empire state building. The waitress instantly knew who he was, showing them to a window seat; the place was deserted.

"Ok what do you need to know?" Alex asked and took out her phone to record the session." Do I need a lawyer?"

"No need, we got CCTV of the attack and they confessed to malicious intent and assault. They have been charged and are due it courts next week. I thought you might like to know." He stated as two glasses of wine arrived and two menus.

"If you aren't taking my statement, why are you here? Do captains even take statements? Alex asked raising a suspicious eyebrow.

"Not normally but then again many captains don't volunteer with the dog unit. I wanted a chance to see if you were ok and get to know you informally. I know Archie was concerned over your welfare." James said smiling at her over the top of his menu.

"Yes, I am sure he was," Alex laughed relaxing a bit.

"You changed your hair again?" He asked, trying to initiate a conversation even though Alex was bewildered and suspicious.

"I like having different looks with wigs without damaging my hair. Shouldn't you be out fighting crime?" Alex tried to change the subject as the waiter arrived. James ordered two burgers as Alex hadn't even looked at the menu.

"No this is my day off I thought I would take you out instead." He replied taking a swig of wine.

"And you are wearing your uniform because?" Alex asked still not gauging what was happening.

"Look at me, I look good in my uniform, also it comes in handy for arrogant boss'. You wouldn't come out with me otherwise. No one can resist an officer in uniform." James smiled and relaxed in his seat as the burgers arrived. *It's a surprise his cap fit on his massive inflated head, but Alex seems to be falling for it.*

"Isn't there something about witness protection or harassment if the case has been closed?" Alex laughed at his boldness. There wasn't one kink in his ego.

"There is but I'm the captain so no one can really say no to me in this precinct, can they?" He laughed taking a huge bite out of his burger, chewing enthusiastically and taking another. He was a fast eater.

"I think you took the exam too early." Alex commented with a smirk and crossed her arms. "What if I say no?"

"Then I will say that you will break Archie's heart." James replied he was half way through his burger.

"He isn't your dog and he isn't even here!" Alex nearly choked on her wine. Alex raised his hand a ball of fur bounced over to her and jumped up to give her a slobbery greeting.

"You were saying?" He asked with a laugh as he finished his burger.

"Tell him to get off," Alex cried through a mouthful of fur.

"Only if you agree to go out with me!" James replied, reaching for his fries.

"Fine get him down!" Alex said. James gave an order and Waffles jumped down, swiping her food on the way, swallowed it within a few seconds and settled on the floor. Alex was left dishevelled as James looked apologetically at her plate.

"So, you were saying that you like to experiment with your hair? What else do you like?" he asks as she pulled the dog hair out of her mouth. He waited patiently for her to continue the conversation. Captain James liked to take control; they talked for so long and she was brought a fresh burger. The clock read four o'clock causing Alex to jump up startling James.

"I need to go back to work. This couldn't happen today. I am so fired." Alex panic flapping her hands around and trying to collect her belongings.

"Don't worry you cannot be fired while being interviewed by a police officer." James said looking bemused by her reaction. Alex pulled some money out of her purse and tear out of the restaurant before he could say anything else. Alex was such an idiot.

The Senator was meeting Katy tonight to confirm the final payment now his name was cleared. She needed to keep her job in order to continue with the plan. There was no time for an actual life. She made it back to the office and ran up the stairs in her heels. The senator is stood next to her desk. *It seemed to be his new favourite office hang out. The sectary must have tipped him off when I was coming back in.* He smiled eerily as he saw her re-enter the office. Alex slowed her pace, holding back her true feelings before she sat down.

"Ahh nice of you to join us." He said loudly. "I expect that you will be staying late to get the rest of your work done. I would hate to dock your pay." She didn't look at him and scowled down at her desk.

"No sir." Alex replied to her desk without putting up another issue for him to address. She started to work and within two minutes her heart sank as Captain James made his way back into the office. *Can't this guy take a hint.* The senator rolled his eyes before going to greet the captain with his fake persona again.

"I'm afraid miss Alex has too much to be getting on with for more police interviews." The senator told him with a wide smile.

"I just wanted to drop this card. It has my personal number on it. She can call at *any time*. Can I remind you of the legislation allowing employees being dismissed from tasks for reasonable police requests?" He made direct eye contact at her as he said this to the captain. With a nod and a smile James left his card with her and turned to leave but she saw him linger at the doorway.

The senator walked over to Alex thinking he had gone and ripped the card into pieces and drops them into the bin in front of her face. The captain watched looking concerned before disappearing out of the door. *Oh crap. If he investigated her work place, she might get identified as not existing.*

 This couldn't be going any worse. Alex kept her head down working on the strategy report. The senator left at around eight leaving her as the last one in the building. Alex had an hour to get to the apartment and get changed. Sacking off the report she hadn't finished; Alex called the car as she ran out of the office. The phone rang. She held it beneath her ear as the car pulled off.

"Yes?"

"Jones there is a cop car tailing the senator."

"What, oh for heaven's sake. That would be Captain James my date. How can I lose him? He seems to have a hero complex."

"I've put a loop on the rear CCTV. You need to use the back entrance then I'm afraid you will need to switch into waitressing clothes and close the bar down. Then you can leave. There will be a waitress who will swap places with you. Her name is Svetlana."

"Is that the best thing you can come up with?"

"It's all we've got. We're watching you but there is a chance you could be compromised. Keep to the plan. There is too much at stake. The senator will get you in with the president. The boss has been very pleased with your progress." The tech guy assured her. The car pulled up at the apartment. "Fine." Alex replied hanging up.

Within ten minutes, Alex was outside again waiting for another car. It dropped off at the other side of the block away from the police tail on Senator Smith. She slipped in the back looking dressed like a waitress with her head down. She grabbed a tray and brought drinks to Smith's private booth.

"I thought you weren't coming." He said looking surprised by her outfit.

"You are being tailed. Someone is sussed on you. I told you to not trust anyone." Katy hissed through her voice chip as he handed her a fat envelope.

"I think I know who that was. I will have them dealt with." The senator replied looking frustrated. Alex's stomach flipped but Katy kept her composure and slid the envelope in her bra. *I have had just about enough of this guy.*

"Don't risk collateral damage. You need to follow the book from now on." Katy instructed. This situation wasn't as fun as it used to be. The senator wanted to continue talking but she excused herself and left him alone. The cops were on the move outside the speak easy; all in plain clothed uniforms.

Alex switched with the waitress who was waiting out the back. The senator remained seated and took out his phone. Through her earpiece the tech guy informed her that he was searching the Cover Girl but nothing would come up. Alex watched from CCTV feed as she left the bar on her phone; Smith was watching the waitress who replaced her. He got out his phone.

"Yes, I am in need of PI who also does intimidations," The senator said into the phone. Alex listened over her phone as the car pulled up. "I need a woman taken care off; blonde, 28, bit of an idiot. Yes, get me some dirt first and await further instruction." *Wow what a piece of trash.* The tech guy was snickering over the phone as Alex rode home.

The senator left the bar and was tailed all the way home by the police car. Alex got out of the car, switching into another one before reaching her apartment. To her surprise there was a police officer walking past her building. He tilted his hat to her and she noticed him speaking into a radio as she walked to the lift. *This is why I don't do the whole dating thing. People just get in the way! If it were me, I'd send some goons after him.*

When Alex got up to the apartment, she went over the balcony to look down at the street. She couldn't see any police cars so instead she went over to the iPad to use the hacking system to track the police cars. There was an undercover cop car parked opposite the foyer door. It had been there for a while with no order to move. This is going to make things complicated.

Alex's work phone rung as she getting into her pyjamas. She didn't recognise the number and turned it silent to set the alarm. It vibrated again in her hand.

"What?" She asked in an annoyed voice.

"Hey, sorry to call so late. I just wanted to make sure that you got home safely," said a warm familiar voice.

"Who is this?" Alex asked confused and then it dawned on her. "Captain James?" Then before he could answer she needed to shut it down so Katy took over.

"Look sir it's late and I need to be in early so I'm not fired tomorrow. If you're going to be a creep and use your police powers to stalk me. I'm telling you now. Let me be. I need to work." Katy said rolling her eyes, hanging up abruptly. *I tried to be nice for Alex's sake.*

The phone didn't ring again but the police car remained. Her tech guy gave her orders to keep him close yet with the Senator being after Katy and the police watching her building it was too complicated. Even though he was handsome, intelligent and charming, she was meant to be staying under the radar. Her stomach twisted a little as she put her clothes away. She had to remain focused, not be distracted by a guy no matter how good he made her feel.

Alex looked at the clock. She needed to be up again in four hours. She blinked and her alarm was going off. She made it in before anyone else. The senator arrived late today but looked directly at her as he went to his office. From her phone she could see him checking for updates about the Cover Girl but the PI hadn't found anything. All the contact information for Katy had been wiped. It was like hiding in plain sight. All she had to do now was move on to the next phase of her plan; The president.

Her phone buzzed with an email titled. Katy Jones – Urgent help required.

Textbook Hero's Complex

Hello, me again. Thought I might as well put in more than just a few comments. I may have led Alex astray from the mission. The email relit my fire; I needed the spark, the excitement of a job. Something that would take Alex away from that… man. I've been living like this for over six months. Why can't I have a little fun? I know what I am doing and that little goody two shoes jaunt with the government services taught me a lot of skills. Time to dust out my Louboutin's. Let me tell you when the Senator was back in Washington, I had my first appointment.

Katy got out of the taxi in her new season Chanel, with a black-haired wig on and glasses on. It'd been a month. Alex had been working hard in Washington, Katy working the crime scene at night; it was killing both of them. Everything was monotonous, they needed some excitement. Today, Katy was meeting a crime boss at the MET gala. This man was in charge of a fuel fraud scandal with a local gang which were being raided tonight. Once the hide out had been cleared off evidence, the feds would be after him for removing stolen goods. His alibi was being at the MET Gala. He was in his forties and very handsome. Katy wore a figure-hugging cocktail dress; the face of a run way model she googled and tweaked a little.

The gala was an annual fundraiser and the fashion event of the season in New York. Alex's outfit wasn't exactly out there but the designer label got them pictured on the run way. Every piece of evidence backed up his time line to the police. They went into the gala; start circulating amongst the crowd with the likes of RuPaul, Beyonce, Rhianna and so many Victoria secret models. The outfits are bizarre, wonderful and took up the whole red carpet with some dramatic wardrobe changes along the way.

What should I call this boss? He is pure blood American. Hmmm Cletus? George, nah let's go for Oliver. He knows everyone. God, I wish every assignment was like this. This sort of party is where I belong. I think I may need to join Instagram.

Oliver got a call saying that the compound has been raided by one of his associates and to expect to be arrested at any moment. They were about half way through the evening. The moment the police came Katy would vanish. One of Oliver's men would have a car waiting for her to leave.

The moment came when the police stormed into the gala. Oliver ushered Katy away as he was approached by several officers including to Katy's annoyance Captain James. Katy froze on the spot and watch as James read Oliver his rights.

As Oliver was being led away, James and Katy make eye contact and for a second Katy thought he recognise her. Thankfully a group of paparazzi blocked his view and Katy was whisked away. Her heart stopped in the car when a thought occurred. Were the dampeners on the settings that allowed him to see her true face? *SHITE.*

The plan was to drop Katy off at the corner; she could get into another car to drive around to the other side of central park. She got changed as fast as she could in the back of the car. Katy reset the dampeners, pulled blonde wig on and messed it up a little. She put on a pair of trainers, running clothes and left the car round the back alley of the office at work. No one was there today.

What was she thinking having no protection? Katy had let her confidence make her take risks. She couldn't message her tech guy as it would be in breach of contract and putting herself at risk. There's no way she can check for cop cars with the iPad being at home. She had a plan to cover her tracks. Katy was the only one in the office so she used the dampener to break into one of the computers; the video footage allowed her watch the arrest and find the opportune moment to leave. The whole gala was under surveillance. Alex left the office several hours later and took the tube instead of a cab so there is video footage and times.

Half an hour later, Alex climbed the steps up to her street and jog across the road to her building. Her heart was pounding from the anxiety; she nearly screeched as an unmarked police car sounded the siren for a second behind her. Her hand shot up to her neck to ensure that she could feel the dampener buzzing.

"I'm so sorry I didn't mean to give you a fright." said a familiar voice. Alex tried to catch her breath, turning to look at Captain James who looked very apologetic. "I just noticed you J walked in front of a parked police car." He looked stern and Alex stared round at the empty road. Her breathing increased making her feel like she was going to pass out. Why was he there after all this time and making a major arrest? She must have gone very white as James grabs her arm. "I was joking," He reassured her, trying to laugh as Alex had a mild panic attack.

"Gosh, I've never been in trouble. I cried when I broke the uniform code in high school," Alex said, feeling nauseas. *This wasn't a lie. Thank God we grew out of the goody two shoes faze.* James thought she was going to pass out too. The adrenaline from the day was tanking. He placed a strong arm around her waist and marched her into the foyer.

"No, I'm fine," Alex insisted despite growing light headed, feeling overwhelming. She hadn't had an attack in a year. It was getting worse and the blood started pounding through her ears; she was sweating. *Come on girl, not in front of hero complex guy!*

Before Alex could refuse, they were in the lift up to the apartment. James led her to the couch and put her legs above her heart and went to grab a paper bag. He muttered gentle soothing things until her breathing returned to normal and she calmed down.

"Wow I really should work on my surprises, shouldn't I?" James said trying to break the tension.

"I'm sorry, I'm under a lot of stress at work and if my boss knew I was in trouble with the police he would fire me on the spot," Alex explained. This was the truth too. If she got charged with anything then she would screw up the whole plan. "Why are you here, were you waiting for me to get home? I told you to give me some space." Alex asked swinging her feet down so she could look at him properly. James looked a little guilty and uncomfortable.

"I know you told me to back off. You are focused on your career. But we had a big public arrest today and I saw someone who reminded me of you. He was let out on a technicality and we have no evidence to charge him. I have the commissioner breathing down my neck about the whole ordeal and I felt like you might be up to talk. Nothing more." He explained sheepishly. Alex could see the sincerity in his eyes. She began to relax. "I'm aware that your boss does not treat you right. Want me to threaten him?"

Told you so!

"No please don't do that!" Alex exclaimed as her voice went high again with anxiety. James closed his mouth as he saw that she was not in the right headspace to joke about anything. He cast around for another topic of conversation. *God girl, you're making even me stressed.*

"This is a great place, have you lived here long? He asked admiring the living room. He must have been wondering how she afforded the rent.

"Just about six months. I moved in after I finished university. This is one of my father's flats so he would be pretty angry if I brought in a lot of friends. He made a contact who got me a job at the senator's office. I wanted to get into legislation but I dropped out of law school." Alex lied but it sounded pretty convincing. Anything could be made plausible with a little bit of hacking of the records.

"That is interesting. I have a townhouse on the upper east side. I've always wanted to see the view from this side of town." He asked, she nodded over to the balcony. Alex got to her feet and showed him out. The sky line could not be more beautiful with a full moon and every star out that night. James felt the vibe between them. In his uniform, he was dazzling in the city glow. *I tried to tell her to behave but Alex seems to supress me a lot better than she used too. I'm logging out this is going to be gross.*

They stared in silence at the city skyline. Alex loved seeing the lights at night; she would make up stories of the people living in the buildings. She sometimes pined for London but New York has its own pull. You couldn't see where times square is from here and she had resisted the urge to go. The cold air blasted them and Alex let out a shivered. James moved closer to her wrapping his arm around her to pull her in closer to his body. It was a sly move.

"I might go in and get a shall." Alex suggested trying to put some space between them. It felt nice to be held and she could sense what he wanted. She wanted it too.

"No need," James replied and took off his officer jacket, draped it over her shoulders and hugged her from behind to warm her up. Alex fit perfectly in his arms. It was like something out a fairy tale, the kind that made her weak at the knees and mind. James could feel her pounding heart beat through their embrace. His matched hers as she rested her head against his chest. He inhaled the scent of her hair deeply. Alex made no move.

They stood there in silence enjoying the view. Yet he didn't make the move either. She had told him to back off so he wasn't going to cross that line. Dam him for being a gentleman; it made him even more attractive. He wasn't perfect though. Alex moved her head to look up at him and he couldn't wait any longer and kissed her.

For such a strong man, he used the gentlest of pressure on her lips. She kept her eyes shut as they started off slow and he pressed her closer to him. All the space between them was gone. He moved his face down to her neck and kissed her gently toward the dampener. She let out a soft sigh and turned round to face him. He pushed her against the railing, bending down to kiss her on the lips again. It was like fire between them as their hands started to explore each other.

Alex wrapped her arms around his neck causing his jacket to slide off her shoulders. James decided he wanted her at his eye level and picked her up and perched her on the edge of the railing while they kissed. He held her tight but she felt a jolt of sanity. *Or was it me?*

"Stop," Alex said pulling away and wrapping both her legs and arm tightly around him and away from the edge. "I can't do this." James laughed and stepped back with her hanging onto him like a koala. She dropped down and walked back into the apartment as the excitement level dropped.

"What's wrong?" He asked, following her back inside with his jacket. "Did I push to much?"

"No, it was amazing but you're a police captain and have political ties. I need to focus on my career and I can't give senator smith any other reason to fire me!" Alex searched for reasons to justify her resistance. Her head was all fuzzy.

"I can protect you from him," James started to say.

"No don't say that. Don't even suggest that. I don't need protection from anyone. That isn't how I roll. It's not the Middle Ages." Alex said. He had hit a nerve and she got defensive. *Finally, she's seeing sense.*

"I get that you want to progress in your career on your own terms but that doesn't mean that you need to work for an ass hole." James replied scathingly. "Why waste your talents with him? I need a media assistant." He suggested. From the expression on her face know that that is the wrong thing to say. He was trying to rescue her. Was she a charity case for him?

Text book Hero complex and stage 5 clinger. Red flag. RED FLAG! Should I say it?

"What get a job for kissing the captain. No. I've gotten to where I am by working not flirting my way to the top." Alex raised her voice and tried to protect her integrity.

I'm going to say it.

"What like living in daddy's apartment instead of your own?" He blurted out getting angry himself. Even though it was utter rubbish Alex snapped.

Oh, I'm going to say it!

"GET OUT," Alex yelled. James started to apologies but she was livid, "Now!" She ignored his pleases and pointed her finger at the lift. He took his coat, pretty sure if there was a door to slam, he would have. Alex was seething.

Told you so.

*Shut up KATY! Mind door slams. *

Maybe I hit a nerve. But I was right! Don't let a man complicate your path, the pretty ones are the most reckless. He did do something right. He got Alex to listen to me. One message to Oliver offering our future services ensured that there was going to be a good flow of work coming our way. I was back, we were doing what she needed. The world was open, there was only the small matter of completing this contract. But it is the greatest assignment we have ever pulled off. Just you wait and see what this woman can do! Without needing a man

Eyes on the Prize

"Jones!" asked the angry voice down the phone. "What is this I hear about the Cover Girl being active in New York?"

"What are you talking about?!" Alex asked wearily. She rolled over in bed to look at the clock; 5am.

"The fact that there have been two instances of criminal bosses avoiding being sent to jail and your police captain boyfriend being humiliated on the front of the newspapers trying to clean up the mess?" He sounded angry.

"That wasn't me!" Alex sat up and stared at the phone thinking for a second, "Well at least the second one wasn't." She laughed to herself but the tech guy wasn't happy. That had been entirely circumstantial but there was word in the crime world that the famous Cover Girl was back and operating in New York. There had been a headline which had stated a woman had been arrested with charges of fraud and being an accomplice to the crime. Maybe there were some copycats *but there was only one Cover Girl.*

So many copy cats had popped up but none of them knew what they were doing and were getting caught left, right and centre. Oliver had her email and she had told him they would need to wait for the attention to die down. There needed to be a distraction, something to draw the Cover Girl's reputation out of New York. All of this was pivotal for the next leg of the plan. Everything was falling into place; the senator was to accompany the president on a trip abroad.

I'm getting to come out to play!

It was a diplomatic trip to China which the president was taking a number of senators with him. As media assistant, Alex would be there to run errands, making her able to disappear into the background. The next part of the plan was in force; Alex was already on thin ice with the senator as he hadn't found anything that could give him cause to fire her. She had actually been contributing ideas which would improve his image. Her discussions with the president's media team had landed him a position in this expedition. All that commuting to Washington had paid off. Though it was actually Katy's tech guy who made all of the accomplishments. However, she took full credit to make herself irreplaceable.

Alex hadn't heard from Captain James since they're falling out. There had been an increase in police patrols in the areas around her building and work which made things tricky Katy. She still had no idea what his deal was. Was it just a normal man likes woman situation or was he suspecting Alex of something? To appear more normal, she tried to lead a more active lifestyle; got a personal trainer to get her in shape before they left done a little bit of sightseeing and met a group of girls for a book club. If he was following her then there would be nothing to report except, she had become addicted to fantasy novels and found so cute book shops to peruse for hours.

The trip to Beijing came around. The week leading up was the most stressful in terms of preparation. There was a lot more security co-ordination. The delegates and their assistants were to be protected at all times. Though on the plane the staff flew economy while the senators had private jets and complained when they were delayed. The president stayed in a five-star hotel. Alex and the other assistants were placed in the much quieter and cheaper hotels down the road.

The media storm is crazy; they were surrounded by reporters from all over the world. This was a momentous event to build bridges between the two nations. The US president was doing it for the image. The assistant's hotel didn't have any media attention. They had one small foyer to work in to get the Wi-Fi. Alex sat working constantly with one other assistant.

Her name was Erin Defraz. She had a Latino background and kept her self very presentable. Of course, the senator's team hadn't had transport arranged for them so together everyone found a way to the hotel from the airport. Alex had sat next to her on the long bus ride and they hit it off. Erin was very friendly and as soon as she knew that Alex spoke Spanish the spent the whole trip conversing secretly. She worked for the president himself, having been forgotten with the rest of the staff.

There was more to this friendship; Erin was going to be the way to the president. *Or at least my way.* Alex planted a dampener which she had reprogrammed to trace her location, technology and listen in on conversations. Their meeting wasn't a coincidence. It was so thin she would never have felt it. The moment to plant it came on the first day. Alex told her there was a spider on her. This was followed by several minutes of her jumping around the room in terror much to her amusement. She let Alex "get it off her" to allow her to plant the bug.

The president was going to be on a tour of some of the mountain villages so they were left alone with an unexpected day off in Beijing. It was nice just to be able to walk around for the day. Even though Alex had lived in New York and London, the pollution of Beijing was on another level. They wore ventilator masks outside and her skin broke out in a painful rash on day one; thankfully the dampeners hid this. They had street food, saw the palace and climbed the great wall before returning back to the city centre. Erin had to leave to go and do some press conference preparation. Alex decided to stay out and prepare for Katy's plan.

Katy went to the nearest designer shop to buy a new outfit all in black and ordered a black car to pick her up. She notified the client that she was on her way. Tonight, was going to be pivotal if the plan was to proceed. Everything had to be perfect. Katy have even hired security for the night. These men had all killed before and would ask no questions for the right amount. Of which Katy paid them double their standard fee from the senator's invoice. This wasn't going to be an exchange of goods. It was going to be an exchange of vital information which would play a big role in things to come. The president was going down.

Yes, you heard me right, bring down the president, that is what I was being paid to do after all of this time. Behind the CIA, FBI and MI5. My boss has the right intentions but I will need to get into that at a later point. Why? I will have to tell you that later...

The car pulled up, two men got in; one next to Katy and the other in the front seat. There was a second car started following them. The cars approached the office which was hidden behind a popular night club. They used a side entrance and the first room which had giant hard drives in an air-conditioned space. All of the machines were on wheels, the cables ran through the ceiling units and lights flashed everywhere. Katy followed the man into a room, sitting down amongst several men and woman working away on computers. The screens were covered in code and their hands flew across the key board. One of Katy's securities were also acting as a translator.

Three people sat at the desk in front of her. She wondered if they knew anything about her dampeners but it would be suicide to point it out. Katy put her bag on her arm, pulling her sunglasses off, flicking her hair over her shoulder and made dead eye contact with the gentlemen sitting before her. *I was in control and looking HOT.*

"Welcome Miss Jones, we have heard about your services and we are thrilled that you are able to join us tonight." Katy's body guard translated from mandarin. "I hope that you will enjoy our hospitality while in our country and anything you need." She nodded to the hosts, adjusting her stand a little show open body language before replying.

"I am very grateful for you being able to see me under such short notice. My circumstances only allowed for a small window of opportunity." Katy replied which was followed by her translation. The language barrier gave an extra layer of protection.

"We would like to use your services and connections to gain access to the president's personal computer. We acknowledge the risk this would be to you personally but you will be greatly rewarded for your efforts." Katy was advised yet nodded.

"I will need some time to gain access for you as I am not close to the president yet. Would you allow a time frame in which I could achieve the task?" Katy asked. The three people murmured momentarily and then offered her three months to achieve her task. "As for my reward, I only require twenty percent of your asking price. The rest I would like to be donate anonymously to several charities." Katy added to the terms. The amount they were offering was preposterous. There was no way she could handle that much money especially if it didn't work out for her new clients. It led ties to her account so it was better to siphon it off to charities who could help those effected by the president's downfall.

"We will head your request and ensure the funds go to the right places once you give us information on where to transfer the funds too. Please take this, once you have access to the president's computer, simply plug it in and turn it on and we will be able to do the rest." The men instructed her and handed a pen drive across the table. Without a moment's hesitation, she slipped it into her bag.

"What should I do with the drive afterwards?" Katy asked to ensure that there would be no trail left.

"The drive will self-destruct around an hour after it has been installed. This will give you enough time to get the drive to somewhere safe. The explosion will be small but ensure that it is in an enclosed container so that it will not pose a threat to you." They gave the final piece of advice. The plan was so meticulously thought out even at such short notice.

"Will you get the job done before the next election?" Katy asked, shifting in her chair as the conversation was ending. Time was passing quickly and she had to get back to the hotel.

"Miss, we operated the Russian interference in the last election. I can show you our portfolio if you would like but then I would need to kill you after. Now, do you have any more questions." Replied the leader threateningly and she knew that this was her cue to leave.

"No, after this we will cease to have contact. There can be no trace of me being here. But as you and my client have the same goal, I do not see there being any need to communicate again." Katy said, getting up from the table. The translator finished talking and Katy left the way that she came. They got back into the car and the security team drop me off at the hotel a five-star hotel.

Each of the security team were handed a green pill which they took with her watching. This pill will not kill them but cause amnesia for the next twenty-four hours. They had been paid enough to not utter a word of this encounter. Katy knew all too well; every man has his price.

Once the car had driven off, Alex changed down a side street and burn the clothes and walked back to her hotel. The media teams were arriving back; tired and weary from the days travelling so she slid into their ranks and went back to her room. After ten minutes there was a knock at the door and Erin came into the room.

"How was the rest of your sightseeing?" Erin asked as she plonked herself down at the end of the double bed. She had chocolate with her. Just the pick-up they both needed after another intense day.

"It was nice to have a break from everything. But the pollution is insane I need to have a long bath to get the smell out of my hair." Alex replied and take a large slab of the chocolate. It wouldn't take long for it to vanish.

"I had to watch the president act like he was Santa talking to children for the cameras and pretending to plant a tree for climate change." Erin rolled her eyes. "All these images were sent back and I had to determine which one painted him in the best light." She told rolled her eyes. She had a few on her iPad and all of the children looked terrified of him. "There is one where he was threatening his assistant with the spade. Have you met Charlie?" She asks.

"No," Katy replied with a smile. It was nice to just have a little bit of normality.

"Oh, he's the loveliest person you will ever meet. There is no one like him in the president's team. He's the junior sectary." She said with an air of dreaminess in her voice.

"Sounds like you might have a little bit of a crush on him?" Alex teased leaning back onto the cushions and smiling as Erin went very red. She talked about him for the next few hours.

Before long she left and they had to be up early for the final day of the president's visit. And soon it was off in the airport again with the memory stick stowed securely in Alex's hand bag. Now it was just a matter of time to get the opportunity to use it.

Remember your training

Alex finished in the office very late one night a couple of weeks later. It was nearly 1am; she had to organise an uber to pick her up at the door. Alex was so fed up of this job. She nearly passed out in the back of the uber; even now she had emails pinging into her inbox. Alex dozed off, her phone on silent until they reached her block. The road is cordoned off by the police.

They were in gridlock but close so Alex decided to get out to walk the rest of the way. There was probably a robbery or something a blockade up as the perimeter was very wide. Alex had to walk the long way round. Probably not advisable at this time of night but right now she just wanted to get home.

It was pretty chilly and the cold winds funnel up the avenues Alex crossed gaining mild relief in the perpendicular streets. Then she heard the bangs of gunshots; over the wind she could not sure from which direction they came from. She ducked behind a car as three men ran round the corner pursued by two policemen. Alex had her gun in her bag and pull it out while staying out of sight. Her heart started thumping as she ran through the training she could remember in her head.

There was further exchange of gunshots and cries of pain. Alex heard the crackle of the radios; a few officers emerged chasing down the gunmen heading in the wrong direction. The street was deserted.

Alex carefully manoeuvred herself so that she could see what was happening. One of the officers was down. A familiar voice yelled from down the street and Alex peeked over the car.

Captain James was giving orders to the crooks, standing in front of his partner lying on the ground gripping his legs. The sirens were getting closer and louder.

"Put the gun down!" James yelled. "This is your last warning." BANG. James fell to the ground in a cry of pain; he and his partner were vulnerable as the criminal reloaded his weapon. Alex knew she had to act. The gunman walked over to him on the ground as she dashed behind the cars to get closer. Her heart pounding as she pulled out the mags, throwing her bag into a bush. Her exhaustion gone as adrenaline filled her veins.

Alex moved purely on instinct as she emerged from her hiding spot. She shot straight at the man's hands causing him to drop his weapon and blood to pour out of his hands. Nick had taught her to be a crack shot; working without protection she had gone to the shooting range for practice. Keeping the gun raised, Alex approached him standing over James and his partner.

"Back up!" she yell trying to get control of the situation. The man's hand was bleeding but he still had a grip on his rifle. He took a few steps away from Captain James who watched the scene desperately from the ground. He was bleeding from his thigh. His partner was unconscious. Alex hoped it was just a flesh wound. Looking down was a mistake as the gunman charged Alex, pulling the gun out of her hand. She had used up all of her rounds already. Alex kicked him off her and remembered her training to win against a strong opponent.

"Don't let him get his arms around you." Alex heard Nick's voice in her head. She hit him hard with the bottom of her hand in the nose and rolled out the way. She got to her feet and ran to get him away from the officers. There was a rock on the side of the road, Alex stooped down to grab it as he caught up with her.

They weren't more than twenty yards from the fallen officers. Alex turned round with the rock in her hand; using it to smash the man in the side of the head. It had little effect and he got his hands around her neck and brought her down to the ground with all of his weight between her and his hands around her neck.

There were shots fired but they didn't hit make contact. Alex's head spun with the lack of air and the noise of more police officers arriving on the scene. The man smacked her head against the concreted and Alex gasped as her head swam. Then a memory flashed in her head. Alex bucked her hips causing him to fall forward, trapping his arm. She got her feet under his hips pushing him away and taking the pressure off her neck. James called out to her from the street. Swinging her leg over she crushed his neck with her thigh. There was one last thing; the dampeners. Alex pulled one off her neck placing it on the man's head and hit it hard to set off the stun setting. The electricity course through him rendering him unconscious. Pulling the dampener off the criminal and replacing it Alex gasped in a lungful of air.

Alex pushed the man's limp form off. She ran to James's side. He grabbed her by the shoulder, his face contoured in pain. The fear and relief in his eyes. Alex pulled off her belt; making a tunicate around his leg to slow down the bleeding. She turned her attention to the other officer. He was breathing but unconscious. Alex pulled his leg up to divert the flow of blood from his calf, he had another would on his arm. Thankfully the officers converged on the scene. James was on the ground pushing pressure on his leg as Alex struggled with the other officer. EMTs arrived to take over as the officers arrested the criminals.

"Alex, I'll come see you as soon as I can," said James on the ground as he was treated. She squeezed his hand before being led away to be examined herself.

The officers were carried away on stretchers as Alex sat in the back of an ambulance being checked over. There was a nasty crack on the back of her head and some bruising but apart from that she had been lucky. She refused to go to hospital again; feeling exhausted she requested to be allowed to go home.

The next part of the night was a blur as the aftermath of the adrenaline and shock took it out of her. She was taken down to the station to give her account of what happened. She had to provide evidence of concealed weapon permit. Captain James was going to be in hospital for a few days as there had been shrapnel which was embedded in his leg and he would need an operation and rest. The dog team were hailed a success and the press were desperate for witness interviews.

Alex was told that she would need to testify in court before she was allowed to leave. The precinct wasn't far from her home. It was nearly five in the morning. She could go home for a couple of hours sleep before going back into the office. Alex was escorted to the exit by two officers to avoid the paparazzi. It took a long time for the car to get through the crowd to her apartment so it was six in the morning before she got to sleep. No point going to bed now as she needed to go to work but her phone rang. It was the senator.

"Hello?" Alex said and walked into her closet.

"Miss Alex, is it true you saved the police captain's life last night." Senator Smith demanded without any form of greeting.

"I wouldn't say that exactly." She replied but he cut her off.

"I have just had a call from the 89th precinct. I want you to take a week off to recover. Make sure you rest up and don't take any calls from reporters. Leave the media to our department." He instructed her and with that hung up. Alex blinked and look at the phone disbelievingly. A day off? From the man who had been a slave driver to get her to quit for all these months. It was going to be used for his political agenda. Alex turned off her phone and collapse onto the bed.

She slept poorly, remaining in bed until the late afternoon. She had to drag herself out of bed eventually to go to the fridge and realise that there was nothing in; not even any left overs. There were a few good places to eat close by. She felt like she needed to go for a run. Without dawning a wig, she laced up her trainers, put on her dampeners and pulled her hair back; leaving the apartment with her phone and cards in her pocket. It was a hot afternoon and she didn't feel like running a full lap of the park so just a couple of times around the lake. Alex jogged back by a Starbucks and walked the rest of the way back with a large muffin and smoothie.

As Alex walked back to the apartment, she noticed that there were a few reporters hanging around outside of the entrance of the apartment.

"Shite," Alex swore hiding behind the corner and getting out her phone to switch out the face on the dampener to get past them. As she approached the building the cameras turned and the reporters rushed over. The women they wanted was blonde and her dark natural hair had shielded her. They turned their cameras back to the entrance as she pressed the button for her apartment and relaxed as the lift doors shut. Alex got into her flat and walked over to the iPad and turned on the secure mode.

"Boss?" She asked as the call was answered immediately.

"I can see from the papers that the plan went off without a hitch!" The boss said over line. Alex relaxed into the sofa and smiled.

"I didn't mean for people to get hurt. But having the captain involved was genius; this story will push the senator to the forefront of the media attention and get me into the office." Alex said. The plan had been in place last minute as the deadline approached with the pen drive but nothing was changing. Katy needed the opportunity to get into the oval office and their options had been running out. The tech guy had sent the officers in the wrong direction. They had used a criminal from James's early career to lure him out on to the street but things had gotten out of hand.

"Everything is coming into place. Once you have used the pen drive, we will move onto stage three of the plans. Keep it up agent. It won't be long before justice is severed that even this president won't be able to sue his way out off or tweet." The boss said and after a few more instructions ended the conversation there.

Alex hung up and went to the kitchen. There had been a food delivery outside of the apartment. She busied herself making something that was going to be substantial that would last a few days. Alex turned up the radio and danced around the kitchen as she cooked letting off some steam.

When the food was finished, she perched side of the counter and ate a portion out of a bowl while the rest cooled on the hob. It wasn't anything special but it tasted amazing. Her self-care routine had gone downhill over the last few months. The lights were off in the living room and she paused to listen. The lift was approaching her floor. Turning off the music she activated the dampeners and grabbed a knife off the counter. Then the definite sound of footsteps.

"I'm calling the police," Alex yelled and peaked over the counter to see who it was.

"I wouldn't bother!" came a reply in the room with her sending a chill down her spine. To her horror there was someone standing in the doorway. Alex jumped up with the knife at the ready and was greeted by Captain James; bandaged up but in his uniform. What the hell was he doing here? And for another question, how the hell did he get into her highly secure apartment? She kept the knife in her hand ready scanning for any sign of an imposter. There was no panic button in the kitchen.

"What do you think you're doing breaking into my flat?" Alex asked furiously. She did not feel welcoming at all.

"I'm sorry I tried calling and left a bunch of messages. I told you I would come and see you as soon as I could, the man in the foyer recognised me and allowed me up. Alex pulled out her phone and true enough there were over seven missed calls from him. So many other messages were popping up, including most of the people in her office. Alex had not been paying any attention to her phone. The media had also been messaging her. The biggest message was an email from the senator office which read;

"Local senator's assistant saves hero cops."

"You should have waited for a reply. You scared me half to death." Alex complained turning the phone over. Her tech guy could deal with those issues.

"I wanted to ask you a few questions about what happened. But I thought you might not be looking after yourself or even be back at work after last night. I was very worried about you and when you weren't answering I thought something might have happened or that you were in distress." James explained, looking slightly amused that she was not the damsel in distress he had been picturing. "Not to mention you saved my life and I wanted to thank you." Something about his demeanour changed. *Oh, here we go again. He's trying to be the hero despite being rescued by a woman.*

"You're welcome. I promise I wasn't stalking you. I was just walking home." Alex explained, "It's nice of you to be concerned but I really can look after myself. That was probably evident last night when I saved your neck. I've actually had a really good day!"

That's its girl, put him in his place. This crap doesn't fly.

"Oh, I know they have already traced your movements from work on the CCTV. You always seem to end up in the wrong place at the wrong time. Maybe I am the damsel in this fairy tale." He observed waiting for her reaction. Alex smirked seeing right through his insinuations.

"Why does anyone need to be a damsel? Are you interrogating me Captain? Do I need my lawyer?" Alex leaned forward and raised an eyebrow questioningly. "Because this is a very creepy way of doing it." Which made him laugh and break his suspicion.

"I was hoping that I could just check in on you before I go home. I need to get some rest before I go back on desk duty. There are lots of reporters outside. I managed to avoid them. Could I crash on the sofa and leave in the morning?" He asked looking mildly pathetic and staring over at her expensive sofa.

This man is going to make me go blind by the amount of eye rolling he causes me.

"Fine, but you leave before I wake up. "Alex said with a grin thinking if she had left the iPad in the bedroom or not.

Why are you falling for it?

*Katy; shut up! *

"I accept your terms." James said and disappeared into the living room. Alex tidied up the kitchen; noticing James had found his way into the shower. She got some things out of the cupboard for him to sleep on and left the room.

The bedroom door was mostly closed as Alex got changed. She kept her dampeners on just in case he came in. Through the crack in the door Alex saw a glimpse of James with his shirt off. It made her jaw drop. He was ripped to high heaven; her heart fluttered. With a groan she jumped into bed and moaned out her frustration into her pillow. There was a soft laugh from the living room as the lights all turned off for the night.

Well, that went better than it could have…

***

Alex woke up half way down the bed and tangled up in all of the sheets. She had no idea what time it was. Alex looked at her phone which she had left on silent; there was a lot more calls and emails. A few from the senator asking her to come in despite ordering her to take some leave. She groaned in frustration. Then the thought occurred to her.

She needed to shower and she couldn't with the dampeners on. Alex walked out of the bedroom, finding her uninvited guest cooking up a storm in the kitchen. Alex would have been annoyed if it didn't smell divine. On closer approach it did not.

"I did try to leave like you asked. But there are still reporters down there. I will get tailed anywhere that might have food. So instead, I thought I would try to make you breakfast while I think of an escape plan." James justified his presence quickly before Alex could talk. There was a major smell of burning and lots of dishes in the sink. He was buttering really burnt toast and looking embarrassed. "I said I would *try,* I didn't succeed. Sorry I just have a protein shake." He said looking apologetic making Alex laugh. "I eat nearly anything but I've got to admit this is a pretty bad." She tried a mouthful, trying to hide a gag and spit it out subtly.

"I need to get some real food in," said Alex, trying to strike up a conversation. At least there were no hidden gadgets or weaponry James could discover in the kitchen. She kept talking as he took a bite out of the rotten toast. "With work and being back and forth from Washington all the time, food just goes off so I end up buying it in to the office to eat. Less cleaning." She smiled understandingly.

"I used to be like that. Then I discovered the joy and satisfaction of making my own meals." James replied, smirked as he saw Alex sneakily put hers in the bin.

"Yes, it looked very appetising." she said sceptically as he put down another charcoal ensemble in front of her. "I prefer cereal anyway. There's too much fat in a fry up for the morning." She went to the cupboard to get the bowl out.

"I notice you only have items on the lower half of your cupboards." James observed pouring some tea and sitting at the kitchen bench to dig in to his charcoal abomination.

"That's because I can't reach very high and I don't like wearing my heels on the hard wood floors." Alex explained at the random observation.

"Ah it's a hard life for the short." He joked. Alex got her bowl out, turning round to catch his eye, as he innocently bit into his food; hiding the expression of disgust. "I assume that there is no one here to fill the top shelves?" He asked unsubtly and the penny dropped.

"If you're asking if I'm still single then yes." She replied sweetly and dug in to her cereal. "But I like it that way. Life is easier and I have the freedom to do whatever I want. But right now, I'm focused on my career and that will be thing that takes the priority in my life right now." This had all been said before and sometime hadn't changed her opinion but certain events coming to play wouldn't allow it to happen anyway.

"That's true. You are still at the same point in your career that you were six months ago. But you have to admit that there is something drawing us together. It might be the universe but you have cropped up multiple times. I have saved your life and you have saved mine. I think it would be safer if we just moved in together to protect each other." He said so matter of factly that Alex almost chocked on her cereal.

"Move in?" Alex asked with an incredulous voice. "I barely know you. All I really know is that you are a high profiled police officer and that you like dogs." Alex replied quickly starting to panic. "Is it that you have seen my place and want to freeload to get the address and I just happen to be here too?" James saw that his little joke had hit a nerve and held up his hands in submission.

"Well, how about we put the brakes on and just start dating instead?" He asks turning the proposal on its head and I frown as Alex saw the reverse psychology, he was putting on her. Classic move to get a commitment phobe on the same page.

"I don't think I will be able to get rid of you any other way," Alex replied and felt her heart slow down. If he was going to be her boyfriend it was going to be a very fresh relationship which she could control.

Dating fine, but he never specified that we were exclusive. Or that I was…

"No but you know women these days. They only go for guys who are super rich with fancy apartments. Oh, wait you already have half of that." James replied with a fake sad face.

"Meh I'm more of a crazy cat lady," Alex joked which made James look offended. "Well, I think that I could get use to a feline or two or a dozen." He walked out of the kitchen and made his way into the bathroom to brush his teeth and came back into the living room.

"Anyway, I think that you should stay at home with all of these cats if you want them. A woman should be at home keeping the place clean while the man goes to work and deals with the day-to-day stress." James joked. Alex swotted at him before he could suggest anything more ridiculous. He grabbed her wrists and laughed. She brought her knee up hard toward his groin. He reacted before she could make impact and used her being unbalanced to his advantage.

James pushed her back so that her knees hit the sofa and made her sit down. Alex put her other hand behind his neck and pull him down with her. What followed was a childish display of wrestling with each participant playing dirtier and meaner; hair pulled, licking and even biting. Of course, that was Alex, James pulled away in disgusted allowing her to push him off her onto the floor.

Unfortunately, she followed and landed on top of him. They grappled for a moment each trying to gain the upper hand while not causing any actual damage. Alex was about to say something; James pressed his lips against hers to stop her. This was the ultimate move. She melted inside at his touch. She reached her arms up around his neck and pulled him closer. The feeling of intimacy was not one that she had experienced for a long time and she pulled herself closer to him. She didn't know how long they were there for but James suddenly flinched, pulling away and griped his leg. The wound caused him enough pain that it broke the pair of them out of the lusty trance. The chemistry had been building up for a while. The pair of the gasped and smiled at each other.

Eugh...I want to vomit!

"I think I am going to go and have a shower!" Alex said, standing up and reaching out a hand to pull James up next to her. He smiled and watched her hurry into the bedroom. She showered as fast as she could and chose her shortest pj shorts and a baggy t-shirt as she came back out to talk about what had just happened. But he was gone. There is a note on the counter which reads *until next time*. That was it. Alex grabbed the phone and tried calling him but he didn't answer. Had something gone wrong? Could there have been something left out which he had discovered?

Got to hand it to him that was a sly move. It enrages me, Alex!

STOP FALLING FOR IT!

**I can't help it! **

You watched Bridget Jones again, didn't you?

**No! Well, maybe. Only three times! **

I'm going to burn that DVD collection; it warps your brain! Time for someone with a clear mind to be in charge!

Katy ran into her room and fished out the iPad and turned it on to the secure line. The tech guy answered after two rings.

"Katy where have you been. The president has put out an arrest warrant for the Cover Girl."

"What?" Katy replied moving back into the living room.

"He wants you brought in. It is a top-secret bounty. I believe this is the time. You are going to be hired by the president."

"He can't do that? It's not the right point in the time line? I haven't even used the pen drive yet" Katy replied, sounding worried. The pen drive was locked in her beside cabinet next to her loaded gun and hidden wine stash.

"Well, if you don't go to him, he might bring in one of the copy cats and you know what will go down then." He replied. Katy took it all in for a second and contemplated the different outcomes. To be prepared for anything you have to think of every possible scenario.

"Let him do it." Katy said, a plan forging in her mind.

"What?"

"Bring in a copycat. A good one. That way we will know what he wants and what he is his motives are. Reduce the risk. Keep the Cover Girl anonymous; an idea. After all, no one knows my face. The Cover Girl could be anyone. As long as I don't use my natural face, I'm safe. Let's use a decoy. One of those people trying to steal my gigs. But we need to choose the right one." Katy thought out loud. Alex had some ideas but she was locked away right now.

"You need to hire them. Test them out." The tech guy replied. "They need to do the job perfectly or he might get suspicious and this might be our only window in."

"Oh, this is going to be fun!" she replied and hung up the phone positively bouncing into the office. Despite being asked by the senator to come in for new conferences she had the week off and this was going to be the perfect time to stomp out the fake Cover Girls giving her a bad name over New York city.

First thing she had to do was go on the dark web and search. It doesn't take long before Katy has three hits of potential Cover Girl copy cats replying to her advertisement. Rookie mistake, let the business come to you. Time to put on the red wig and break out the heels.

*Can I come out now! I promise I've calmed down. *

Maybe in the next chapter sweetheart, go watch Bridget Jones; the edge of reason while I have some fun...

There Is Only One Cover Girl

Now let's break this part down. This was an exciting time. Not only was it a time to take down the copy cats ruining my good name. It was a way to evaluate the client experience. Yes, I was conducting market research. A business woman has to take every opportunity to improve her service. I might cut in here a little bit as this was maybe the lowest point in my career. There is only one Cover Girl; if this is the experience people give, I'm surprised anyone is hiring us at all anymore.

Contestant 1

The first copycat called herself Katie Jane, *I don't know how she got the name wrong*. Katy thought she would shake it up and was dressed as a man; full suit, boobs tucked in and the dampener providing facial hair. Her voice chip was reprogrammed to give her a deep voice. She played a drug boss want to avoid a raid at one of their hideouts. They wanted to hit a club down the town and got photographed with the Cover Girl as an alibi. The tech guy managed to give some false information into the police so that she would be interrogated and see how she coped. *It didn't go well.*

To start with she was very late. The woman was in a heavy set and in a tracksuit. *For a club.* Not the glamourous women advertised. The night was bitterly cold and she was sweating. They nearly weren't allowed entry into the club. She sat down after ten minutes without engaging with her client. Katy had sent over fifteen emails determining the detail of the evening and she had only replied to one asking about when she would get paid.

They left the club early and only got a side photo coming out of the club behind someone famous. This wasn't planned it just happened to work out. *I got the impression she was acting like a baby sitter and hadn't had any real clients.* She asked for the money and Katy said she would transfer it as soon as the appointment was over. *Rookie mistake, take the money up front in an anonymous cryptocurrency account! Amateurs.*

If she had read that in the emails or signed a contract then she would have learned exactly what could happen and what was expected of her. They parted ways. Katy got home, wait for an hour or so before setting up a fake call. The FBI are called her in. She was asleep and had no lawyer when the police came. Katie was pictured accompanying a known felon into a club who was busted for cocaine dealing and was thought to be the director of the operation but wasn't present on the scene and she was the witness. The woman was arrested for aiding and abetting a crime when she couldn't validate the story and tried to confess to being a con artist. *I didn't pay her for that experience and I did not feel sorry for her.* She learned her lesson. She got off lightly but never moonlighted as the Cover Girl again.

That was fun!

Contestant number 2

For the second appointment, Alex played a female who was a tax evader for a huge public firm. This was based off an email that had requested the real Cover Girl back in London fell into the trap of hiring the non-professional. *It's their own fault what happened. I won't tell you who in case I get sued but they have been brought to justice.* Katy and the Cover Girl had dinner at the plaza and then went on a tour of the natural history museums something anniversary. It is a highly publicised event. This time the Cover Girl who turned out to be a man called

Charles Jones; who by the end of the night was revealed to be a highly intelligent stripper with a lot of class and sass. *That was a surprise. I liked him.*

Much to Alex's surprise, he took her out and did everything by the book. He even had his own security. Charles was charming, witty and banterous. He did like to talk about his past clients; relaying what would have been confidential information. However, Katy planted a knife on him as he entered the museum to see how he would react to being arrested. It didn't go well. He threatened the security guards with it and got arrested himself. *I might need to take the blame for that one but he really hadn't prepared for any eventuality so I had to do something to knock out the competition.* As the contract was not fulfilled then Alex didn't have to pay him. *Some of these copy cats are just pathetic.*

I may have gone to check on his at the club that he worked. The black eye made him look more attractive in my opinion.

The final participant

Katy didn't hold her breathe for the final girl. After the last two disasters the last plan was a little outlandish. She might as well drive out the rest of the competition. This plan was going to test every scenario that might be faced with meeting the president. There were actors, stunts and more surprises in store.

Katy was disguised as a low-key business woman and waited in times square to be greeted by the Cover Girl. A woman walked up behind her with security guards. Katy turned round to see Rose smiling at her. It took a moment or two for Katy to take in her face. Somehow, she managed to keep her face placid though her heart raced with excitement. She was dressed to impress even just for the dinner.

"Miss DeFraz?" Rose asked, Katy nodded. "My name is Katy Jones. I am here to ensure that you don't get into any trouble. I hope you took in all the small print on the contract. This is Junior; he will be keeping us company tonight." Katy nodded again. This was going to be an exciting night. "I thought we could start off at the jazz lounge and then go to the theatre. It's the opening night of SIX." She suggested and when she didn't respond led the way out of times square. Katy silently followed her into the jazz lounge. It was a large classy venue which had a lot of famous faces round it. This was beyond Katy's expectations and she felt rather underdressed in her plain outfit of trousers and a smart blazer.

Junior got them some drinks as we sat down in the centre of the club. He disappeared for a while. Eventually Katy found her voice. She hadn't seen Rose since she had come to see me on the Azores when Katy was getting back control of her life. She was the only person who knew what Alex did for a living and now she seemed to have stolen her identity. Katy wanted to make her sweat a little to see how much she had learned from watching Alex as Katy over the last few years.

"How long have you been in the field of work?" Katy asked hiding her smirk behind a glass of wine. Katy's disguise had Rose fooled but the image dampeners were so effective that she would never have second guessed it.

"Oh, a while, I don't really keep track." Rose replied in an impassive tone and stirred her drink. Rose didn't really have the knack of engaging the customer and they hadn't confirmed conversation points before so her execution was flawed. Katy decided to turn up the pressure.

"So, were you behind the murder of the Prince of Monaco?" Katy asked quite bluntly waiting for Rose's reaction. Rose blinked and looked uncomfortable but answered the question.

She could tell that the security would be watching me closely so Katy needed to be careful.

"I'm not sure where you heard that but I can assure you that I had nothing to do with that. Jones is a very common last name." She replied without giving any hint of insincerity.

"I was recommended your services by my friend Brady. Have you heard from her lately?" Katy probed while the jazz music starts to play. This was a name drop that wouldn't prove to be very useful but it would show if Rose had done her research.

"No, I'm sorry. Clients don't usually give me their real names but I am sure I would recognise their face." She said. Katy didn't give up and loaded a photo of Brady on her phone and showed it to Rose. "No, I have never met her before." She cut off the conversation. Rose was beginning to get annoyed, the corner of her mouth always twitched when she was irritated. She was swirling her glass a little too hard. Katy laid off for a while changing the subject to the weather and let Rose calm down a little.

"It's time for the raid." Katy said looking at her watch a while later. "The board meeting will be beginning without me." Rose had become a little hostile from all the questions. Katy knew that she would see the evening through to the end. They left the club and as they cut down 36th street, a van pulled up next to them. Several large men got out and grabbed both Rose and Katy. The next thing they knew, the van doors slammed and they were driven off. Rose's security couldn't do anything but chase the van. One of them yelled out but it was muffled by the van doors. If she had done her preparation then there would be a tracker on her person for them to follow.

Rose had her head covered and arms tied behind her back as they drove through the streets to the docks. Katy was quite comfortable in the back of the car with a seat belt and chair.

She ruffled her hair a little to look dishevelled as Rose swore at the kidnappers from under her hood. She threatened about a tracker and her security but when they reached their destination there was still no sign. The van skidded to a halt. Rose was dragged out. Katy pretended to make protesting noises and we both get placed on chairs in the middle of an abandoned tool shed.

"Where is the money Defraz? demanded one of the abductors pulling Rose's hood off and yelling in Katy's face.

"I don't know what you're talking about?" Katy pretended to cry in fear but she was really trying not to laugh.

"You better talk or your friend here is going to get a lot less pretty." A second man said pulling back Rose's hair and raising a blade to her face. The panic was evident in her eyes. The actors were really committed and Katy might have over done it a little but to be fair she had gone through this as the Cover Girl a few times so Katy needed breaking in.

"She has nothing to do with this. Let her go!" Katy yelled and the lights went out. Katy let out a fake scream and the actors added an extra layer of fake blood. Of course, they weren't going to actually hit her. Her stage management and direction skills came in handy sometimes. "I told you, I don't have it." Katy gasped as the lights came back on. Rose looked in horror at Katy looking beaten and bruised.

"She's right she doesn't. Because I have the money." Rose pipped up taking everyone by surprise. The man holding her looked blankly over her head at Katy for direction.

"What are you talking about?" Katy gasped through the fake pain.

"Leave her alone. I have the money." She continued. "I'm sorry I went behind your back. I was going to let you know as soon as the raid had taken place." Her expression was concrete but her eyes told me to play along.

"Fine we can get rid of this one." The first man said and dragged Katy away out of sight while she screamed in fake fear. This had turned into improvisation.

"I will tell you where it is if you don't hurt her." Rose yelled.

"You better start talking." The man said as Katy was "beaten" out of sight. This was proper improvisation. They pushed and pushed her but Rose wouldn't crack. The blind fold was put back over her head. At that moment, Rose's security arrived. Five people ran into the building with real guns and chased the actors away. Katy had warned them this might happen. She had staged gun fire simulations set up from the roof. They were all blanks. The security shielded us both with the bodies and got us out of there before they could find out what was happening. Within minutes we were flooring it back to Katy's flat.

"Come with me," Katy said as they rushed out of the car and into the lift. Her security swept the apartment before Rose sat down. Her demeanour was so strong, Katy couldn't believe she would have sacrificed herself for a client. Even if it wasn't true, she had bought enough time to allow help to arrive. It was going to be a risk but Rose had proved herself to be the one for the job.

"Tell you security to wait outside the door." Katy instructed, taking control of the situation. Rose snapped her fingers and everyone left. That gave Katy a flutter of pride as she had her security that tight in the resort. She pulled out the iPad and blocked all radio and phone transmissions.

"I'm very impressed with how you handled tonight. I need to be honest with you this was a test. I know you are not the real Cover Girl." Katy said, putting the iPad down and standing up turning off the voice chip via her phone. Her voice lost its accent.

"How do you know that?" She asks standing up behind me. Katy waited a second before replying, her heart beating hard in her chest with anticipation.

Do you promise you can keep your cool?

**Yes, let me out you monster. Look what you just put her through! **

She was fine and coped well. Ok take the reins. I need a break.

"Because I am the real Katy Jones." Katy replied in her London accent. Rose gasped. She pulled off her wig and turn round to look at Rose in the eye. "Otherwise known as Alexandra Shaw." Her face is astonished as Alex's natural hair fell down to her waist and for the first time in months, she turned off her image dampener. Rose blinked heavily as the disguised disappeared and smiled at her with her own face. Rose stared at her.

"Alex?" She asked hesitantly and reached out for her face as if she couldn't believe what she was seeing.

"It's me," Alex replied and she felt the tear pierce her eyes. A sense of relief and joy washed over her.

"But you died?" She asked her voice shaking. Rose was shaking so hard as they grasped each other's hands.

"There was an attack. I was told about it. A client approached me just before and I had to fake my death though. I have a job to do. No one knows who I am except you." Alex explained as they hugged as tightly as possible and sank onto the couch. Alex broke away. "Why are you being Katy? Do you know what happened to me? The reputation I have in the criminal world. You could become a target."

"I know but I had to keep katy alive so that I could feel like you were still with me. I did everything you used to do. Even with the security team, Junior is really the guy from the Azores you assigned to me." She explained her eyes lighting up as she talked. "Oh, Alex the rush of the job. There's nothing like it." Rose nearly squeaked and squeezed Alex's hands.

"Why are you in America." Alex asked after they hugged again. It was like no time had passed between them.

"Oh, I'm getting married to junior in Vegas next week. I just saw the ad and I knew there were some copy cats around so I thought why not earn a little extra money on the way." Rose said excitedly. Alex rolled her eyes at her. Of course, Rose would do anything for a chance at a great shopping trip.

"Well, there's another reason for you to stay a little longer. I need to hire you for a big job." Alex proposed, waiting for her answer.

"Tell me about it later but first things first. I want you to come to Vegas with me as my bride's maid." Rose asked shutting down the business talk. This took Alex by surprise, triggering her anxiety. She stood up and walked round as she thought.

"Rose I can't. I have an important job to do here." She replied, running her hand through her hair.

"If you're saying that there is job out there for the Cover Girl then wouldn't Katy just set it up around her own schedule?" Rose pointed out with a sly smile. Alex opened her mouth to reply and shut it again.

Dam she got you.

That was the best argument Rose could of said but she had a boss this time. After all, she had been working so hard for the last nine months. Alex could just say that she needed more time to recover from the shoot out to the senator and tell the boss that she needed to train the new Cover Girl with a job in Vegas. Alex started giggling and got her phone out and to call her office and the boss. She just remembered to turn on the voice chip before Senator Smith answered.

"Miss Alex?" he replied on the second ring. "What can I do for you?" He asked.

"I'm sorry, I don't think I can come in this week I need a little bit of time to get my head straight." Alex said in a weak, vulnerable voice. She could hear the annoyance in his breathing down the phone as she finished. Alex paused to hear the outcome smiling down the phone. "The journalists are wanting an exclusive interview when I return with the both of us explaining what happened." She added. That sold it for him.

"Take another week and then I need you back on the team." He said, Alex made a gulping sound in thanks down the phone and hung up before he could say anything. Rose started laughing but Alex raised a finger as she pulled out another phone and hit the dial button.

"Hey," she said as the boss answered the secure line.

"I found our girl!" Alex said with jubilation as Rose stifled her laughter in a cushion.

"Excellent, we need to book her in with the president." The boss said down the line. He seemed very relieve after the last two disasters.

"I need some time to get her ready. This is going to take some planning so put her in for next Monday with the president."

Alex said and she make eye contact with Rose. "Also, I'm going to be away this week. I've got something personal I need to do. Things have gotten a bit heavy. The van assault was a bit of a trigger for me." Alex lied through her teeth.

"No problem. Go and recharge. Just keep your dampeners on at all times," He instructed her, hanging up no questions asked.

"Well, that was easy," Alex screamed in happiness dropping the phone on the couch and spun round. "You know what this means?" she asked, jumping on the coffee table.

"VEGAS!" They screamed hugging each other and jumping around.

What happens in Vegas...

I've got a confession. This was my first real holiday in years. It's going to get messy!

They left the next day. Rose went back to her hotel to pack up her stuff. *Junior turned out to be Elliot from my old team.* Rose introduced us as long-lost friends she had bumped into in the street because Alex couldn't risk him recognising her. He had first had experience working under the real Katy Jones.

A couple of his friends were meeting them in Vegas so Alex organised a limo and a private plane once they reached JFK. No lines. No security. They drove right on to the runway. *Time to spend all that danger money in style.*

Rose was earning a lot of money recently but nothing compared to what she was going to earn when she worked for Alex. Rose had a tiny room booked for six people with only two beds in the Venetian resort. Alex was gobsmacked to hear that she would need to squeeze between two or three men she had never met and sleep right next to a newly married couple on their wedding night. These weren't even her peers; two of the party had worked with Katy, it was like sharing a bed with the help!

Alex made a call on the plane; they were met by a car when they landed four hours later in Vegas. The car didn't take them to the Vancian but to the penthouse suite at the Bellagio. With the view of the Eiffel tower and the famous fountains from the balcony which could see each end of the Vegas stripe. The penthouse had been booked out by some actress. *Lindsey Lohan? I think but my fifty-thousand-dollar upfront fee got her kicked out of there for us.*

Alex smiled as she saw Rose and Elliot's face drop as they entered their luxurious accommodation for the trip. They're faces dropped; running and screaming like children exploring the suite. Then turning their energy on her, the had to catch her so both of them hug Alex so tightly she couldn't breathe. She was nearly roped into planning the honey moon as well but Alex said she would rather leave them to that themselves. Elliot's brother stood at about six foot five, he hit her so hard over the shoulder in gratitude, she nearly faces planted off the edge of the balcony.

Elliot was handsome, sweet and ripped. Alex had grilled him on the plane ride over and he had answered every question perfectly. In return, she had a little explaining to him about how Rose and herself had accidently bumped into each other on the streets of New York. The dampeners had been reprogrammed several times over the last few days to keep up the disguise. The story had been agreed that Alex was a wealthy widow to one of New York richest but sadly, ancient bachelors. It saved some painful questions; after four bottles of Krystal there weren't any more.

Rose and Elliot were getting married the next day so Alex decided that today was going to be Rose's hen do/Elliot's stag, they would all meet up later. She even gave them a budget to hit the town. Rose relaxed as Alex did some organising before the alcohol started flowing and all control would be thrown out the window. There had to be some subtilty. She ordered stylists for today and tomorrow, wedding dress appointment and a spa treatment. The stylists came up to get us ready while we gorged on room service. Rose was refusing to eat anything except dessert which Alex was too happy to comply with. Once Rose was ready, they headed down the casino floor to hit the slots, feeling like supermodels. Heads turning in their direction as they strutted through the casino floor, their heels clicking in sync.

There was one problem; they weren't quite sure how to play black jack. Alex hadn't played since Monte Carlo and that had all been set up. Today was just about having fun. Safe to say they didn't win big but the large bets attracted some attention as the most distinguished people on the casino floor. The drinks kept flowing as the staff waited on their every whim. They were free pouring the spirits causing the girls to get sloppier so Alex ordered water to have a bit of a breather. Then a better idea popped into her head. She whispered into ear of one of the waitress's and slide a tip into her hand. Five minutes later they went out to the front of the hotel to our own rolls Royce waiting outside.

The car drove them to one of the smaller hotels where they got out. Rose covered her eyes; when Alex removed her blind fold, they were sat at the front row of the Magic Mike strip show. She screamed so loudly with excitement that the crowd around her joined in with a mixture of laughter from Alex. Magic Mike had always been one of her favourite films. This was the closest experience you could get to the movie. Rose was given a money gun so when the lights dropped and the crowd screamed, she made it rain on the stage before anyone even came out.

The dancers jumped into the crowd and they were both given specific attention by each dancer. The one who looked like Tarzan had the best abs Alex had ever seen. Some girls got pulled up on stage and Rose looked at them with utter jealously yet she was enjoying herself. Alex pulled one of the dancers down off the stage. As he grinded on her she gave him a small wad of hundreds with some specific instructions. The MC came onto the stage and announced that there was a very special woman giving up her freedom tonight so it was their duty to make sure she knew exactly what she was missing out on.

Three dancers appeared out of the wings and picked up Rose's chair and carried her onto the stage. They pretended to worship at her feet as the music built. Each took their turn spinning her round in their arms and grinding on her to the cheer of the crowds. Rose had never looked so happy. Alex got her phone out to record because she knew that if Rose didn't have any evidence of this night, she would disown her forever. Alex cheered as the lighting changed and the music's beat dropped.

One of the dancers appeared on the stage wearing a black cloak and a phantom mask to the theme song. Rose nearly fainted with glee; the secret fantasy's we had both shared had come to life. The phantom actor had her on her chair and slowly got undressed on top of her until there was nothing left but the cloak and the mask. Beneath which they both disappeared to the cheers of the crowd as the music hit its peak. The cloak was whipped off to Rose wearing the mask in the arms of the most beautiful man Alex had ever seen. Rose was breathing heavily. *God know what happened underneath that cloak?* He carried her off the stage in a fireman's lift, placing her back in her seat. Alex grabbed her arm as Rose melted into her seat staring at the dancer. However, this time, Phantom dancer offered his hand out to Alex as the music changed to a slower beat.

Another woman brought up onto the stage opposite her. She was placed on a seat and the stage went dark. The dancer started moving around her and grinding slowly. The dancers swapped and squealed in delight as Tarzan came to approached her. Alex was picked up and spun around on his hips, feeling every inch of shredded muscle of the man. *I can't explain how exhilarating the feeling was. To be in public and allowing this beautiful man to be gyrating over me.* The dance finished with Alex and the other participant carried half way up the stage scaffolding with both of them clinging on for dear life but laughing. Tarzan carried her back down the stairs and placed her next to an equally sainted Rose. He slipped her a card and blew a kiss before he went back up on the stage for the final dance. Those eyes made her insides flutter.

The crowd did not stop cheering even after the dancers had left. Rose and Alex needed a few minutes to find their feet. They had their own little photo shoot with the men which Alex would never show anyone but let's just say the photo of her splitting over them is framed somewhere.

They got back in the car to head back to the Bellagio hotel to go to the Hyde bar in front of the fountain waterfront. The most expensive, exclusive club in Vegas. They guys were already seated and incredibly rowdy. When they saw Alex and Rose arrive, they were guided through to the suite which had its own bottle service and balcony for the fountains.

The music was booming in time to the fountains and they were all watching them. Rose and Elliot were snogging and sharing stories about the fun they had had. Elliot had also been to a strip club but after the night Rose had she had nothing to say. Alex watched the fountains; disappearing into her own happy world for a minute until her phone started buzzing in her bag. She got it out and walked down the steps to the fountain edge before answering.

"Hello?" she yelled into the phone not recognising the number.

"Hi Alex, it's James. I'm just at your apartment with pizza. I thought you might want to hang out seeing as I hadn't heard from you all week. But the concierge said you were out. Should I just wait?" He asked barely audible over the music.

"I'm in Vegas right now." Alex replied hesitantly. She must have been slurring a little as it was hard to tell with the champagne fog in her brain.

"Vegas? Why are you there?" He asked with a shocked voice.

"Marriage." Alex yelled as the fountains started up again. She turned to watch in awe a bit like a magpie distracted by something shiny.

"Alex, what?" James replied but Alex felt the drunken emotion welling up inside her. Tears pricked her eyes at the colours illuminated the water. She cried; "Yes," down the phone. All of a sudden, she felt so free and alive. It was so perfect and overwhelming that this was her life. The tears of happiness rolled down her cheeks as the champagne haze got worse.

"Alex, you're drunk? Are you alone?" James's voice asked concernedly as the fountain started to sway or was that her. She put the hand with the phone down to grip the wall as a wave of nausea replaced the euphoria. She bent her knees to find the ground before she fell and felt a pair of arms grab her around the waist.

"Woah there. Let's get you back on your feet. You need to walk down the aisle tomorrow," said a voice from next to her. James's voice said something on the phone but Alex hung up and looked round to see Elliot's brother with his arms round her. She didn't know if it was the alcohol or the fountain.

Freedom was all she felt. It meant to be. Alex pulled his face down to hers and kissed him hard. He was holding her up so had no way to avoid her surprise affection but he didn't resist the invitation. He was so tall, Alex had to stand on the top step to reach him. He swept her off her feet, placing her on the railing as they ran their hands through each other's hair. The spray of the fountain sent chills as Elliot leaned in closer. Exploring each other as he held her firmly from falling into the water. They finished as the fountain ceased. Alex pulled away; smiling, breathing heavily. They walked back up to the rest of the party pulling him behind her. He seemed confused but happy.

I don't actually remember the rest of the night. I know that I was not thinking clearly but something happened which was out of this world and I woke up in bed with Tarzan from Magic Mike. James and I weren't exclusive, we're free to enjoy ourselves.

Tarzan woke Alex up at around ten in the morning and said good bye as he sneaked out of her room. She had been put to bed last night as they moved the celebration up to the suite. God knows how he had ended up at the wedding celebration. The hangover was excruciating.

Thankfully the happy couple had been separated so they wouldn't wake up together and start off their wedding with bad luck. Alex ordered room service to keep the guys happy while she and Rose had the spa appointment in ten minutes. They crawled there in their bathrobes hoping the relaxation would cure the headache; they got full body massages, nails, hair and makeup done as well as a hearty breakfast after drinking on empty stomachs. They were offered champagne but the thought of it made them heave from the night before. Once they were ready the hangovers had been replaced by excitement and tears.

Thankfully Elliot and Rose weren't going to a tacky chapel to get married. Alex had a local dress boutique bring a selection up to the suite. Rose had chosen a very simple dress originally but Alex wanted her to have the magical bride moment. Instead, Rose chose a figure-hugging mermaid dress with the most elegant train and backless. Alex started crying when she put it on. This was the point; she accepted the champagne to deal with the fact that her best friend was getting married. When the stylists had finished Elliot's, brother came down to meet them, giving Rose his arm while Alex ensured that she didn't trip over her elegant train.

Rose and Elliot had wanted a simple ceremony; outside at sunset so Alex pimped it up a little. They had chosen a Cher efficient. *Rose wanted it.* There was a live band waiting on the roof top of the hotel all to ourselves as the sunset over the mountains. Alex sorted out Rose's dress as she prepared to walk down the trail of rose petals and candles. *Clever right.* The band started a rendition of "Evermore" and Rose linked her arm with Elliot's brothers who gave Alex a cheeky wink as they walked down bathed in orange sunlight. The light shimmered of the subtle diamante on Rose's dress and twinkled like the tears in Elliot's eyes. The photographer captured the happy moment as Rose reached Elliot and Alex sorted out her dress. Elliot removed her veil and she whipped the tears away from his eyes.

Elliot's brother accompanied Alex over to her chair as the music slowed for Cher to do her thing. She noticed someone watching out of the corner of her eye. A man in a shirt and jacket. His hair swept back watch the ceremony from just out of sight. Her heart skipped for a beat when she recognised Captain James. Did she have her dampeners on? What on earth he was doing there? Alex couldn't deal with him as the couple read out their personalised vows.

Elliot promised to pay attention to the little details and clean up his socks. Rose promised not to get mad over things that he did in her dreams or forget to give him all the love in the world. He promised never to hurt her except when he tickled her to make her laugh and she promised never to cook as it would burn down their house. Everyone agreed with knowing looks as Cher declared them husband and wife. The band started up and they had their first dance to Cher singing as the last surprise arrived.

The scene was cut by the noise of a helicopter landing on the roof to take them to their next venue. Elliot lifted Rose into her seat. Alex put on a radio when she had her head set and she look over with both a look of thrill and surprise.

"Well, you wouldn't think I would let you walk to the party! I will see you guys soon!" Alex yelled waving and the rest of the wedding party all took cover. The helicopter took off to do a scenic tour of Vegas with the newlyweds. The groomsmen were clapping each other on the back and they were about to head down to the after party in a casino down town. Alex and the rest would need to get a ride to Vermont street for the casinos for the next plan of activities but she needed to talk to James first. Elliot's brother hung back despite her trying to get the guys to go ahead without her. He compromised by at waiting by the door. He stared menacingly at James and kept flexing his muscles.

This was all a little nerve wracking compared to last night. They weren't exclusive but even I still felt a little guilty at seeing him unannounced. Eww, is this what feelings cause?

"What are you doing here?" Alex asked reaching him in the last of the orange light, giving him a hug. New York felt like it was another world or lifetime. Being herself, no restrictions or planning had left her off guard.

"Your phone call last night. I thought something had happened to you. I was worried when I heard that voice saying you *had* to walk down the aisle" James said, reaching out a hand to touch her hair. "You look breath-taking. I thought you were making a rash decision and getting married." He said with his eyes glowing in the low light. Alex moved his hand away as her image dampener was hidden in her hair but he could see her real face anyway. "You should have told me your friend was getting married."

"What? You flew all this way to stop me walking down the aisle?" Alex asked with a huge smile. "I'm sorry it was all a bit last minute."

"If that's what it took." He replied. "I know I wouldn't of forgave myself if I hadn't tried to stop you but it turns out I got the wrong end of the stick.

"I am here for my friend and that's it." I replied reassuringly. "But I need this weekend for her and for myself. I hope you can understand that with all that has happened." Alex explained gently, she didn't want to push him away but the plan was too important even with this short break.

"I understand. I just wanted to show you that I am here for you no matter what." James said and she could tell that he meant it.

"I appreciate it more than you know. But just for this week I have to look out for my friend. Can you respect that?" Alex asked and give him a kiss on the hand. "How did you find me?"

"I just flew here and told the driver to take me to the most crazy, beautiful girl in Vegas." He grinned and Alex looked at him questioningly. "Also, your credit card is registered here. I have a few friends in high places. It's not hard to miss out on the high spender in town." He smirked and continued. "Don't get up to too much trouble." He finished.

Before Alex could reply he grasped her face between his hands and kissed her passionately. She wrapped her arms around her neck and felt her legs go to jelly. Then as soon as it started, he let her go with a smile and walked away leaving her shocked, wanting more.

Well played sir. He knows how to keep you on the hook Alex.

*Shut up! *

Don't feel guilty, we can't all be heartless monsters like me.

**That's true, you are a mythical bitch sometimes. **

Aww thank you.

James slid past Elliot's brother as Alex walked over to look out the view of Vegas from the edge of the rooftop, her spirit somersaulting. *I know I was pushing away the real thing but this week I needed to have no obligations, no boundaries and no rules.* The sky lined was breathe taking and she thought she could see Rose's helicopter flying around. Alex shivered as the sun disappeared behind the mountain range and the city lights shone. The pale orange being replaced by neon shimmering lights of every colour. Elliot's brother came to join her and offered Alex his jacket. Throwing all caution to the wind. He scooped her up in his arms, planting a kiss on her lips but they broke apart, breathing heavily.

Now this guy is a player, I like him. My turn Alex.

Time for the after party....

The wedding party got to Fremont Street, meeting the elated couple who were a little windswept. Everyone was going to zip line down the length of the street to the casino including Rose in her dress. Alex had her camera out taking as many shots as she could as Rose flashed everyone in the street below. These casinos had higher chances of winning than in the big hotel but it didn't quite line their pockets so with their small winnings and hit the best burger joint in town which has burgers the size of their head's. Rose was given a poncho so that she didn't ruin her dress but Elliot was the one who needed it smearing cheese right down his front. Then back to the Bellagio to get changed into club wear and hit the rooftop bars.

Elliot carried Rose over the threshold of the suite as Alex and the groomsmen followed them in. Alex couldn't get Rose out of her dress as she was clumsy with her fingers but they eventually managed to switch into their short bodycon dress.

The club was huge with a VIP area overlooking the dance floor. *Of course, I had secured us spots in there with unlimited drinks tabs.* There were professional dancers all around them. Rose and Alex headed straight onto the floor while the guys got the first-round drinks. The crowd was mixed with younger and older people with the men outnumbering the women five to one. The music was proper dance anthems. Once the guys called them over Rose and Alex left the dance floor squeezing through the crowd to get back to their booth. After a couple of bottles of champagne, they headed out as a group to dance high on the bubbles.

Rose and Elliot got carried away dancing and act as if the world isn't there having a proper bump and grind make out session on the floor. Alex switched between the guys having the odd spin and grind but as the champagne kicked in; she was quite happy finding her own space, closing her eyes to the music and just feeling the movement and enjoying the moment. With a little too much gusto in a turn she tripped over her own foot and Elliot's brother caught her around the waist. Instead of letting her go again go he spun Alex closer to him and started leading her in some salsa moves. It took her a second to get the rhythm but she was pressed right up against his muscular body and staring into his eyes with a coy smile.

Rose and Elliot broke apart next to them breaking the enchantment. The guys went to get more drinks while Rose and Alex went to the loo. They needed to touch up our make-up and of course Rose had a gush about how much she loved Elliot and this whole experience. There might have been a cheeky tear and long hug which made them spend longer in the bathroom than anticipated. The guys were out of sight and the club seemed even busier as they left the loos. Rose pulled Alex back onto the dancefloor.

One of the podiums with the poles was free which made her face light up. She dragged Alex over to them; started dancing climbing and spinning to her hearts content, her skirt letting her manoeuvre around the metal. They had secretly taken a pole class in London and learned some risqué moves as a pair.

The crowd started watching and cheering as they finished their routine and slid down to their feet again. The professional dancers returned to the podium as the girls returned to the normal dance floor but this time, they were alone. The attention was a lot more intense. Alex and Rose were dancing happily on their own. Alex did a spin; the second her eyes left Rose there was a guy touching her and moving in close. The classic divide and conquer strategy.

Due to her bubbly haze; she assumed that it was Elliot and allowed the stranger to continue. Alex tried to warn her but she was side-lined by another man who separated the pair of them Alex couldn't see past the man. He was pushing her toward a dark corner of the dance floor.

"Hey sweetheart. I like your moves. I love a flexible girl. I know some moves we could try that would involve me and you. How does that sound?" Alex let out a noise of disgust only causing the man to chortle. The guy held her firmly around the waist his other in her hand trying to explore her skin. She ripped her hand out of his grip and tried to slide underneath his arm but the trapped her between himself and the wall. "I didn't say you could leave." He said threateningly, running a finger down the side of her face. He was taller and built so there was no way Alex could push him off her without causing some harm but her movements and sounds were slurred due to the alcohol.

"Get off me." Alex warned in a low clear voice, shoving his hand away but he leered in even closer. She pushed him away with both hands and tried to escape sideways but he was too big. It took all her strength to keep him at arm's length, to stopped his face from reaching hers so he went for her neck instead. Alex pulled her hand back and hit the man in the chin with the heel of her hand. He fell back hard on the dance floor. Alex stared at him for a moment and at her hand thinking she had super powers until Elliot's brother pulled the man up and punched him squarely between the eyes.

Elliot and the rest of the group had retrieved poor Rose after seeing them getting separated. Alex had disappeared. Alex yelled something, pulling at Elliot's brothers arm to get him off the man. The guy was bleeding from his nose and looked quite terrified. Elliot's brother let her pull him off, returning to the had to group moved as a unit back into the middle of the dance floor. The lads formed a protective circle around Alex and Rose. *You could practically smell the testosterone in the air.* Rose danced the rest of the night with Elliot glued behind her looking menacingly at anyone who touched her except Alex.

Rose pushed Elliot off for a second to dance with her and the second he was off her, another stranger smacked Rose on the butt. That was the fuse that lit the fire. He pushed Rose out the way and started threw a punch at the unfortunate passer-by face. Their friends squared up against each other and a brawl started with Alex trapped right in-between them.

It was a bit like being in a violent mosh pit being shoved around and elbowed. Rose tried desperately to reach Alex through the fists but she kept being pushed back by the guys. Alex managed to avoid being hit as the bouncers descended on the party as blood was drawn. Alex was scooped up into a fireman's lift and carried away from the mass much to her relief. The bouncer took her out of the club and set her down at the entrance.

Another appeared carrying Rose who looked more relieved to be out than Alex.

"We saw that you were caught in the middle of that and wanted to make sure that you weren't hurt." They said and then they went straight back in on the radios. As Alex's party were the most important customers the aggressors were thrown out and the police contacted. The wedding party encourage to move to our suite with their compliments and a private DJ would be set up there shortly. *It wouldn't be a real wedding without at least one fight.* Rose was furious at Elliot for losing control but Elliot's brother's *Josh* had stopped it escalating even further. Elliot was a little over protective but he meant to defend Rose's honour.

They reconvened in their suite. Bottle service resumed by the private pool. They decided to continue the party until the sun came up. Alex was still very drunk so decided to take her shoes off. Elliot and Rose made up very quickly and danced by the side of the pool. The other guys had brought some girls up to the suite and were beginning to pair off. Alex was left with Josh even though she had been enjoying dancing by herself by the pool without the fear of being molested. He came over to dance with her while everyone was busy together.

"Are you ok?" He asked as she moved in time with the music.

"Yeah, it's not the first time that's happened. It was my first fistfight though." Alex replied doing some sort of hula dance.

"I'm sorry. We didn't mean for it to get so out of hand. "I thought Elliot had pushed you two out of the way. We stopped after we saw the bouncers carrying you out. I thought for a second one of you had been hit." He said keeping a safe distance.

"Oh no that was just my knight in shining armour." Alex replied, slowing her rhythm as the music changed to some Ed Sheeran. He tensed beneath her at the remark.

"I thought that was *my role* from saving you from the...oh my god did he bite you?" Josh asked moving the hair off her neck. Alex felt it with her hand feeling it tender to the touch. "It's all bruised." she felt it in disgust.

"That bastard. I'm going to go and teach him a lesson." Alex said as the irrational irritation washed over her. Josh laughed as she even started to move away from him so he scooped her up into his arms so that she couldn't go anywhere.

"I think you won't find him now." He laughed swaying to the music.

"I will find away. The staff are at my beck and call. I bet he is in the medical centred." She stated loudly looking around for someone to order around. Everyone else seemed to be preoccupied. Alex had excused the staff so they could sleep.

"Ah I know you are forking out the bill for this trip. I was going to ask what you do but I am a little afraid of you right now." Josh admitted spun fast to make her dizzy. The annoyance was waning and being replaced with nausea. She wrapped an arm around her neck and pulled herself in closer to give him less leverage. Something hard in his blazer dug into her ribs uncomfortably but she didn't mention anything.

"Thankyou." Alex said in the quiet period after he stopped spinning them.

"What for?" He asked as they swayed to "Thinking out loud". Rose must have requested the smooth playlist.

"For helping me with that creep. I am a strong independent person who can handle anything but I'm not afraid to accept help from anyone." Alex recited and Josh started laughing again.

"You are very welcome. I've got to admit when Elliot saw what was happening to Rose and you weren't in sight. We got her back. Rose looked close to tears with worry. She kept saying you should have gone back to the booth. It was hard to find you as your so small then I saw you on your own and that man trapping you I got angry. Before I knew it, I was pummelling that guy." Josh said, his arms tighten as he admitted it.

"Why did you get so angry? It's unfortunately a regular occurrence in clubs." She asked in return. Josh kept the motion while he thought about the answer. The sun was rising and bathing the suite in orange light, even the pool was shimmering with the reflection of the sky. A complete circle for the celebration.

"Elliot and I have a sister and when she was seventeen and sneaked into a club. She was attacked and it took her forever to recover from it. The police never caught the guy. That's why we started fighting those bastards." He explained, Alex could tell that it was a big deal for him to share this with her. The memory was hurting him and he moved a little faster.

"Josh." Alex gasped as his arms constricted around her ribs. It took him a second to notice what he was doing and let her go straight away, setting her down on her feet.

"Sorry," he said with sincerity, his hands reaching around her face as she breathed in deeply and he pushed his lips against her. This kiss was different from the one before, they connected and sparks flew between them. Alex reached her arms around his neck as he pulled her body closer to him. Their hearts pounding against each other's as the adrenaline pumped.

Elliot cried out next to them causing Josh to break away. Alex paused in place keeping her eyes shut feeling the blood fire through her veins.

Bang, Bang BANG.

Josh pushed Alex into Elliot's arms who was suddenly behind her with Rose pulling out the gun which had been hiding beneath his blazer.

Someone had got into the suite and had let of shots right at them. Elliot pulled them away, keeping their heads down as Josh returned fire. Not sure of the target, Elliot threw the three of them into the pool as a shot rang out over head. They submerged into the cold water as the bullets cracked the tiles where they had been standing. Alex head emerged from underneath the water but Elliot kept their heads down behind the tiles and braced them against the edge of the pool.

Several more shots rang out. Rose flinched with each one. Alex tried to squeeze out of Elliot's protection but he wouldn't let her move. There was yelling as the banging stopped. She heard Josh's voice but Elliot kept them in position until they heard "CLEAR". The groomsmen came over and pulled them out of the pool. Josh was standing over a body bleeding into the floor. The red sunrise illuminated his blood-soaked clothes. Elliot was pulling at their arms to get somewhere safe but Katy took over.

"No, get Rose somewhere safe." Katy instructed and bent down next to the man, ignoring Josh's pleas and check his pulse. The man was dead, she took out her phone to take his picture and send it to her tech guy.

In the meantime, she took out the hit man's phone, pressing some buttons on her and hold them together until the devices and download the contents onto hers which she went through quickly and dialled her tech guy's number.

"Hi, I've just had a hitman. Not sure who the target is. You can access the phone information from here. "She instructed typing away on her screen.

"On it." He said, already typing away down the other end of the line.

"There was target for the Cover Girl. He was to bring her in to the president with no other witnesses. Yup it's not you. It's Rose. I'm sorry but we need to move this forward. The president doesn't take to being ignored." Her tech guy explained working his magic, loading everything on her screen.

"Well, I'm not going to give into bullying." Katy said angrily down the phone. "Send an encrypted reply to him. I don't care what it is. Envoy, body, computer virus just put him in his place." She instructed.

"Fine but I won't be responsible for his actions. For the love of god put some dampeners on Rose and keep your gun on you." He said and hung up. Her gun was in her room, the police were arriving so leaving Elliot and Josh to deal with them she slipped into her room and load up the glock, hiding it at the top of her thigh. Katy opened her computer and programmed her spare dampeners and set them for Rose and slipped into her room.

"Rose," Katy said, slipping in and shutting the door behind her. She was sat on the bed wrapped in a dressing gown looking shaken. "Look the police are about to arrive but I need you to put these on and not take them off." Katy instructed and put the dampeners on behind her ears. She set the controls to Rose's phone as a back-up. No one in the wedding party will recognise your but this is going to keep you disguised and safe.

"Who were they after?" Rose asked looking in the mirror at her new face. They were going to need to get her a wig as well.

"They were after you." Katy replied getting a hair brush and pulling her hair back into a bun. "There is a hit on a woman who successfully conned a police investigation in New York."

"Oh, good! I thought for a second that someone knew that you were alive. I couldn't live with herself if I blew your cover." She spoke with a huge sigh of relief. Katy couldn't believe how calm she was.

"Are you not scared?" She asked finishing her hair and pulling a wig over the top which looked passable.

"Not when I am with you and Elliot. I told you he knew what he was doing. But I told him no guns today so I guess it's a good thing that Josh was packing heat instead." Katy nodded as there is a knock at the door. Elliot popped his head in and was followed by Josh.

"The police want to talk to you Rose." He said giving her a kiss on the forehead. "Are you ok?" Elliot asked in Katy's direction.

"Yes, thanks to your fast reactions." She replied with a smile.

"Just doing my job," he replied with a wink. Katy's look questioningly at Rose but she was ushered out of the room by Elliot leaving Katy and Josh alone. His demeanour had changed a little; he was on edge.

"What did you do to the body?" He asked bluntly. "He could have been hostile."

"I was checking to see if he was alive." She replied non clamantly. She was still messaging the tech guy without looking up at him. Annoyed that Katy wasn't paying attention to him, he tried to peek over her shoulder but the phone shut off automatically when someone else was looking at it. Another smart feature she had installed.

"I know who you are." He said as the screen lit up when he looked away.

"Who is that then?" Katy asked and finished her business and looked up at him.

"You are the real Katy Jones. I do security for Rose. I know the story. Rose and Elliot only told me a little about the scheme. You are the legend who died last year." He said sounding more impressed than angry.

"I don't know what you're talking about," Katy replied approaching him and trying to distract him with a kiss. His hand reached into her hair, turning off her image dampener. She pulled out her gun instinctively and turned her face away to hide it. This was a mistake as he pulled her wrist away from her face; tried to look at her in the eye and his other hand pulled the gun away. Like Arya Stark she dropped the gun into her other hand and stuck it against his ribs looking him dead in the eyes with her own. He stopped moving and raised his hands over his head.

"You have a lovely face." Josh said in a calm and amused voice. "I'm not going to hurt you or tell anyone." There was nothing else for it, she was compromised.

"I can't let you go after seeing my face." Katy whispered putting her finger on the trigger but Alex couldn't do it. Not after everything Rose had done for her. A moment of weakness. He felt her hesitation and a second later the gun was out of her hands.

Instead, Katy raised her hands and struck. Against a six-foot four muscular man there is little impact she could do. In one move, he had her in a choke hold with her arm up her back. This was the position Nick had told her never to get into. His arm pressed hard on her wind pipe; he could break it like a twig.

"I know there's a bounty on the Cover Girl. But it isn't on you. You are free. My sister-in-law however is not and I hear you are hiring her to help you with whatever mission you are involved in. I don't think this is wise and you know what I told you about our family. If we turn you instead with her face, then we can protect her and get a handsome reward not to mention gain access into your assets." Josh explained quietly into her ear and pushed on her wind pipe enough to make her feel light headed. The prospect was exciting for him then suddenly the pressure released.

"But I wouldn't do that to you. You are Rose's family so you are mine too. We look after our own." Josh let her go and straightened his suit jacket. "Let's talk business. If we are going to protect the pair of you then we will need to collaborate." Josh said. Katy stooped down and pick up her gun, holstering it in under her skirt. Her cheeks burned with anger; he just demonstrated why security was a good idea.

"How do I know I can trust you." Katy asked putting herself right and turning the dampeners back on. "Why do you think I have to pretend to be dead. It will only take one mistake to ruin my entire operation. I can have you taken away and put into solitary until my mission is finished."

"Then why did you come to Vegas?" He asked which left her silent for a moment.

"Because Rose asked me to." Katy said. "I would do anything for her. Even risk my own life."

"Then you know why I you can trust us. That is exactly what we would do for Rose and her family. You are now part of that." Josh said. Something else presses on her mind.

"This doesn't mean we are together. I don't date. Life is too complicated." Katy said stoutly with her hands on her hips.

"Are you sure, I've seen a different side. What about that man from last night? What about our connection?" He questions her. It was true Alex had gotten close to people recently but this was Katy talking, two sides of the same coin. "This is a lifelong offer of protection and collaboration. No matter what happens. I would never pressure you into anything but I can't deny I won't keep flirting." Josh warned her and closed the distance between them and kiss Katy hard. Maybe her first one in a long time.

Dam he's a good kisser. God this is going to get messy. Now I see why Alex is always getting distracted. Bloody men!

By Order of the President

A week later, Alex was in Washington with Senator Smith. It had been a long week of press releases. Smith had used her image as hero who'd saved the captain for a press boost. Considering she had taken two weeks off it hadn't made much of an impact. She hadn't seen anyone due to how busy she was running the show behind the scenes. Alex met Erin for lunch; she told her about how she had visited several countries following the president on his state visits and trying to boost his image. She wondered if the dampener was still on her.

I will need to come back to the importance of that later so don't forget.

The president was meeting the Cover Girl on Friday night. Both parties had very strict meeting terms; it had to be on presidential property and both had their own security requirements. There was a discussion about whether Alex should be present, however the execution wouldn't work if she wasn't there as there was no recordings or evidence that the meeting had taken place let alone a set of instructions.

Alex dressed up as a female body guard as she was too short to be a believable male body guard. Elliot and Josh would make up the Cover Girls' entourage, all wearing dampeners. They were going to meet in a conference room and Rose would be an interviewer. This was going to be highly confidential.

They entered the white house grounds by a private car sent by the president to be driven in. Rose was in the back and they sat around her.

I would like to highlight the importance of appearance. Katy Jones has standards and when she is meeting the president those standards are Prada.

Alex had to order some clothes for Rose so that she would look the part. What was funnier, her face when Alex shown her the items or when she told her to keep them after.

They drive up the towards the white house and enter round the side; no trace of identity was to be left behind, fingertip gloves, hair nets, dampeners, personal trackers and brand-new clothes. Katy made Josh look like superman on the dampener for her own amusement but he couldn't see what he looks like. The tech guy hooked them up with some gizmo which let them hear the conversations through the wall.

They escorted Katy (Rose) into the building. They didn't go into the oval office but down the stairs to a bunker. The president was waiting in there for Katy alone. Rose glanced back at her entourage hesitantly before entering. Katy nodded to her, giving her a second to regain her composure and walked in closing the door behind her.

Katy was anxious as they stood outside the door staring at the walls and avoiding eye contact with the president's team. But the gizmos could hear through the bunker wall. There was a mini bug attached to Rose inside which projected it through the walls.

Don't even ask me to explain how it works. That's why I have a tech guy.

"Thank you for coming to meet me. I have been most eager for your arrival," came the presidents voice through our mics.

"I came at my earliest convince. I didn't appreciate the messenger you sent." Katy replied, without beating around the bush.

"I wanted to make my intentions known. I did not instruct the man to shoot at you. Just to pass on my compliments but I should have known you would have protection with you. You were very obvious flashing the cash in Vegas. It would have been harder to find you if you had kept it low key and not fund it from your drug camp in Bolivia." The president replied scornfully. Katy felt her blood boil on the other side of the wall. It was an effort to keep her face still.

"Well, I assumed as you have the best secret service in the world that it wouldn't matter how I behaved you would still be keeping tabs on me as soon as I responded to your request." Katy replied smartly, making Alex smile.

"Yes, your reputation proceeds you. I heard of the heroic effort you made for your country before faking your own death. But the Cover Girl has been copied. Your reputation is heroic in the crime world, I thought you might reappear at some point. You are talked about even in the highest levels of security. The woman who fooled the secret service. Unfortunately, I am in need of your very delicate services." The president started to explain.

"I will stop you there. I will not be your fall guy for whatever dodgy scheme you are up to or to get you out of some shady deal that is going to make the rich richer. I do things very differently these days. I need to be rewarded for my efforts and my influence is now back stage rather than in the lime light. That is the difference between me and the amateurs you have already tried." She said boldly. The president seemed shocked.

"How could you possibly know about that?" He asked. Katy had been bluffing but it had worked with a little bit of suggestion had revealed half of his efforts already.

"I have some very smart friends; you should choose your aides more carefully. While I have been inactive, I have been making very useful connections. You know everyone's loyalty has a price. I'm not going to be brought down by anyone again. I want to make that clear before we discuss anything." Katy stated, she knew the president was going to agree to any terms that she set.

Outside, Katy signalled to everyone that she going to be leaving for a moment. Time for the second half of the plan she hadn't shared with the rest of the team. She still able to hear through the head piece but it becomes distorted as she went up the stairs. She got changed very quickly when her tech guy told her where the blind spot was and changed the dampeners to the face of Erin Defraz. The real woman was away but Erin had access to the president's office.

 Alex brought in some forms to be signed and leave them on the oval desk which has his laptop ready. The tech guy covered the cameras giving her under a minute. She took out the memory stick given to her in Beijing, plugged it in and turned on the power.

This wasn't going to take long and didn't need her to hack the computer. She still glanced nervously over her shoulder at the cameras as the seconds crawled by. Who knew what would happen next but the light on the memory stick lit up to indicate it was finished? Alex pulled it out.

The minute was up. She now had an hour to get rid of the pen drive. Katy/Rose was wrapping up the interrogation and her time slot was disappearing. The tech guy instructed her back to get changed and reset the dampeners. She slipped back down into the bunker as the president and Katy was ready to leave. The pen drive growing hot in her pocket.

"I will await your instructions Mr President. I require your *business transaction* before we proceed. Please remember everything we have talked about." Katy made the emphasis on the last word as the meeting wrapped up. The president and Katy emerged from the room. As quickly as they had arrived the entourage left the white house.

The others didn't know what Alex was up to but the best thing to do now was get them as far away from the white house as possible. The president looked quite frustrated as they turned to leave. He frowned at Alex the security guard for a second as their entourage left out the back of the house. The president's car was going to drive them to the drop off point and then Katy was going to take over.

The other three were to change and get on a plane to England. Alex needed to get back to New York to plan out the next phase and to do a tonne of work for the Senator. But he had out grown his usefulness. Alex could finally quit that awful job however, she needed to debrief with the boss before anything else happened or if she needed any extra cover.

"I need you guys to go straight to the airport." Alex instructed her team as they switched cars at the drop off point. "Get out of here."

"No wait, that's not part of the plan. We're a team." Rose said as Elliot looked uncomfortable. They didn't have time to waste.

"I'm sorry. I need to know that you are safe. Take Katy far away from here and keep a low profile." Alex insisted having made this plan prior with Elliot. "Go back to London; make an appearance occasionally then vanish again.

"But we know exactly what the president is planning. If he finds out then we won't be safe." Rose pointed out. The risk was too great, they had to leave as much as it pained Alex to be alone again. She couldn't put them at any more risk.

"We will go." Elliot said over Rose who had opened her mouth to argue further. He turned to Rose. "This is too dangerous especially after what happened in Vegas. Let's go home and start our lives together. Let's have a normal life for a little while. We have the money now."

"Exactly," Alex agreed. "Katy has a price on her head. I couldn't stand it if something happened to you because of me." she implored Rose. The pair of them interlocked fingers as tears pricked her eyes.

"Fine," She replied, "But as soon as all this is over you have to promise me that you will come home!" Rose pleaded with Alex, "you have a life in London!"

"I will try. I won't promise anything." Alex said as tears pricked her eyes. They opened the car doors but before she got in Rose gave Alex a hug. It was the hardest good bye yet. All her new outfits and gifts were mailed back home. Elliot gives me a bone crashing hug and got in the car. They had a prepaid card to get them anywhere they want. The first car drove off leaving Josh behind.

Wow! That nearly had me in tears.

"What are you doing?" Alex asked, resetting her dampeners "Go with them and get the next flight home."

"I'm going to stay and help." Josh replied with a hint of determination in his voice.

Oh god another body guard telling me what to do.

"No, Josh please don't make this harder than it is." Alex replied not meaning to convey so much emotion with these words.

"I knew you felt the same way." Josh said and grabbed the sides of her face to make her look at him. It was more forceful than anything.

Alex, you seem to attract the same type of guy. We don't have time for this.

"Josh no, we had a great time but I don't feel anything for you and my life is too dangerous to think about someone else's safety." Alex explained softly, trying to ease his hands off her.

Yes! That's it but meaner this time.

"Let me help me. I can protect you." Josh said, which triggered a flashback of Nicholas beaten and scared in her mind. Never again.

Oh God! Don't fall for it you are not Bridget Jones!

"No, Josh, No." Alex exclaimed trying to pull herself away but he kisses her instead. This time she was sober but good lord was he a good kisser. Instead of pulling away, she let him crush his body against hers. Then her mind snaps back and Alex squirmed out of his grasp. "Maybe in another life but I can't risk anyone else's life or break anyone's hearts to protect them. I can't do it." Alex was trying to be nice but he wasn't getting the hint as he puts a finger to her lip and hugged her close.

Ahh, I see what you're doing. I'm going to enjoy this.

"I know your scared but there's nothing wrong with asking for help." Josh said, Alex closed her eyes for a second and then open them again with exasperation. She reached up to turn on his dampeners and pulled out her phone, pressing a button on the control screen. The electricity surged through the dampeners tasering him. It only lasted for ten seconds and left the dampeners useless with no data and Josh was out cold. It might have been a bit harsh but it would send a clear message.

Cheering Yes girl that was heinous. I don't even want to take control now. *Fist bump*

Time to start afresh. The last car carried Josh away. Alex took out her phone to get another car. When she got home to her Washington DC apartment, she tipped the driver to get lunch and leaves the USB stick in the car with her old dampeners and phone.

Goodbye shitty apartment!

Around five minutes later the car exploded at the bottom of the street along with all the evidence. She found a new car to ride to get a lift the long way back to New York. But when she reached her apartment, she opened up her new phone and called James's number. There was more to him than previously thought and he might come in useful in the next phase of the plan. She had been thinking about it in the car.

*We might even need to *boke* get serious...*

"Hey," Alex said when he answered. "I know its late but I had time to think about how you came all the way to Vegas to check up on me. I want us to try. Let's go out properly." She said without any introduction, she knew he was playing it cool but she could hear the enthusiasm in his voice. Alex hung up shortly after.

That poor man didn't know what he was in for but upon reflection, neither did I...

Someone Else's Dream

Once again, Alex was in New York alone in her massive empty apartment. This time it felt more isolating and saddening than before after spending time with the closest thing she had had to a family in years. She spent more time with the TV on or playing music because the silence was uncomfortable and let the worries in her head run unchecked. Alex deep cleaned the place; sorted out the kitchen, restocked the ammunition and cleaned up all of the weapons. She had a few concealed on her at all times with a tracker in a necklace and watch.

The boss wanted her to remain in Senators Smith's office as he may still be useful to them though how Alex didn't know. She would be back to the torturous job later that morning as she got up early unable to sleep in the quiet room.

She got out the iPad and make a call to her tech guy. It rung a few times as it was still very early. He answered right before she was about to hang up.

"Hey…I was waiting for your call." He groaned down the line stifling a yawn. "Did you get it done?"

"Yup, bugs are planted, the president has a face to put to the name which isn't mine. It's all *perfect*." Alex replied down the phone, sprawling out on the couch.

"What's wrong?" He asked hearing her dejected tone.

"I'm just a little tired that's all." Alex lied even as tears pricked her eyes.

"Remember why you are doing this. I knew that holiday was going to be a bad idea. You got distracted." He said, but there was a hint of sympathy in his voice.

"Yes, but I'm lonely. It hurts. This all sucks sometimes." She replied harshly, shutting her eyes for a second so that she could take control of her temper.

"Well suck it up. I will give yourself a moment to get ready and the boss is going to be on the line." He instructed, this time making her open her eyes and wipe away the tears.

"What directly?" Alex asked shocked.

"Yup now listen to me. This is going to be tricky. I'm using a load of different VPNs and phone lines." He said clacking on his keyboard. Alex sat up on the sofa and adjusted her hair before the screen lit up with the connection call.

"Sir," Alex said down the camera to the boss. His video was blurred but she could hear his voice very clearly. He had such charisma even with just his voice.

"Miss Jones. I would like to thank you for you work and sacrifice for all these months. I know you have been struggling with it. But I implore you to keep going." He started off the conversation which Alex nodded to in response to keep control of herself. "Now on to the task in hand. You have received your orders from the president. Please give me as detailed brief as you can. Every detail is key for how we approach this next."

"Ok," she replied and started relaying the plan she had over-heard during the interview. "He didn't go into too much detail of the past but you were right. There were some irregularities in the polls. He shouldn't have become president. But he wants to switch Russia's target to China. If there is a threat to North Korea from China and he manages to frame the inference from Russia. He can get a war between the two without risking an expense to the American people. They will target each other's industry and fuel reserves and draw the fire away from our side of the Pacific Ocean."

"Thus, the American economy will race ahead and China will go down. The American shares will soar and he will set up secret supply chains to both sides to keep the war raging on. His companies will benefit and he will keep his sponsors happy. America can only benefit as long as the war doesn't back fire on them. He highlighted the importance of confidentiality as he can't be associated with the frame. That's why he needs me." She paused before moving onto the next part.

"Next week there is going to be a climate change summit with all the heads of the nations at the UN office. The president is going to be there but he needs me to plant an item on the Russian president. This will be traced by the Russian and North Korean satellites when everything kicks off. Then make a distraction to give him as much media exposure as possible when the bug gets switched on. He will be controlling the whole thing from the pentagon. He has access to the system inside the oval office. However, I planted the bug into the President's system so they will be able to work out the what his plan is. There will be no way to trace it back to me and I have a plan of who to use as a decoy when the shite hits the fan." She finished explaining. The boss thought to himself for a moment.

"And you are prepared for this. Once you have finished in the UN that is going to be the end of phase one. China has access to the presidents' files; when shite hits the fan, they will be able to find the evidence they need to find a cease fire. It will all be unravelled when the time is right by Russia and China. But we won't grant them access until the pivotal moment. This all has to be timed perfectly. You are going to need to disappear completely. Then I will bring you back in for the second phase. Your body double will need to use every security procedure as well. We can do this. The wheels are in motion, there's no going back. Let's save the world!" The boss said sounding excited down the phone.

"The girl I've planted the bug on who has been leaving a trace around the world. Will they be protected?" Alex asked thinking about all of the strings that were left untied.

"They were met at the airport and taken into safe custody but she isn't aware that anything has happened, just the president working her even harder. I can guarantee as long as the plan is executed precisely, they will have nothing to worry about. If we get caught and I mean all of us there isn't much that I can do for them." He replied which indicated that every move was going to be imperative. They discussed what would happen if something went wrong; what to expect and to do. *If I told you those details, we would be at the end of the story.* There was one relief in the second phase of the plan; he hadn't said that she needed to work for Senator Smith anymore. She looked up at the clock and noticed the time.

Of course, she was running late for her date. Alex put on some comfy clothes, tied her hair up and placed on the new dampeners and ran out of the apartment. James was waiting for her at the entrance to the park. He gave her the biggest bear hug which lifting her off her feet before they walked into the park.

They walked arm in arm; Alex might have felt a little nervous walking around the park in the dark but tonight was a full moon and the park was bathed in a blue silver light.

"Tell me everything about Vegas." James said as they strolled toward the lake.

She told them as much as she could about Rose and Elliot, creating a story of a life she had long ago before moving to New York for her career. She missed out Josh, the fight and the shootout but apart from that Alex made it sound like an ultimate girl's weekend. He asked her about the guy waiting for her in the door but she brushed it off as a friend making sure she got to the reception. He looked pretty relieved.

But then again, what happens in Vegas stays in Vegas...

She did however tell him about the magic mike performance. He was very good humoured about it and asked Alex for details of her personal dance. They did a whole lap around the lake by the time she had finished her story.

"It's so nice to hear you so happy." James said. "You seem to be a little more refreshed than you were when you left." James said as we took a pathway through the woods towards the boathouse.

"Sometimes I get so wrapped up in work I forget to make time for herself and what I enjoy." Alex pondered out loud. "I haven't even been to the theatre in a year." She admitted slipping up on her cover story for a second. It reminded her of London and all of a sudden, the homesickness grew and she missed Rose more than ever. She didn't want to let James see her tears so Alex offered to race him down the pathway towards the water. The path was lined by the lights; winding through the trees as the space opened up to a massive fountain next to the lake house fountain. Alex's heart pumped as she passed the fountain ahead of him and pelted round the side of the lake.

Now I'm not saying I'm extremely fit or fast but what does it say about the New York police department if one of their youngest captains was beaten by a tiny woman.

Alex was ahead as they got closer to the boat house. They were neck and neck; Alex just taking the lead not knowing if he was letting her win. She pushed herself that last little bit…Right before she touched the wall of the boat house; James caught her by the waist and swung her around in the air stopping her from winning. They laughed hard as Alex tried to touch the wall from his grip. They both gasped to catch their breath back.

"If I was a robber, I don't think you would have caught me," Alex laughed between gasps.

"Why do you think we have police dogs?" James pointed out. To be fair he was still recovering from the gunshot wound but it had only been in the side of his leg and he had been walking the day after. He looked like he might throw up from the effort of the run. "They would have had you in seconds." He said, suddenly hoisting her over his shoulder to her squeal of delight. "I'm arresting you right now before you can get away." He said and walked off. Alex tried to get down but James hopped the fence to the lake and sneaked into one of the rowing boats that had been left out.

"James what are you doing?" Alex asked as he stepped out, pushing the boat out onto the water and hopped in. "Are we allowed to do this?" She sniggered as he pulled the oars out from underneath the bench and put them in the holders.

"No but then again; I am a police captain," James said and flashed his badge from around his neck. He sat back on the bench and crossed is arms with a smile as they drifted in the water. "Well get rowing." He said, nodding at the oars.

"What me?" Alex exclaimed looking astounded.

"Yes, you were determined to run away and prove who is the fittest. Let's see how strong you are." He said knowing that would provoke her. He leaned back to look at the stars. Alex placed both hands on the oars and started rowing. It was a lot harder than it looked. At first, they just started going in circles and then she gained enough control to start pulling them through water and without looking where they were going straight into a tree. Alex ducked out of the way and James got a branch in the face. After she stopped laughing, he took over by switching seats which nearly knocked her into the water.

He took them under bow bridge to the open water. The moon was reflected in the water and the skyline lined the tops of the trees. It was exquisite. There was no one else around. It felt like they were alone in the city. Even the sound of the sirens was drowned out by the gentle wind rustling the trees. James wasn't looking at the view. His eyes were glues to Alex's face. She looked round at him and he reached out a hand so that she could join him on the bench. They leaned in to kiss but there was a light dazzling our faces and yelling from the side of the lake.

"Crap," James said covering his face from the light.

"You said it didn't matter if we got caught." Alex snorted as he grabbed the oars and pushed her back in her seat

"I was joking I could lose my job." He said in a panicked voice.

"Oh no what should we do?" I asked as he started rowing towards the opposite bank.

"When I say, jump in the water and swim for the nearest jetty. I will distract them and meet you at the castle." James instructed and rowed us as close to the bank as possible. "Ok go." He said before she was ready.

"No, I'm not going to..." Alex started to say but was cut off by James pushing me her into the water. *I don't even want to describe to you how that water smelt let alone tasted.* James rowed off in the opposite direction as Alex desperately struck out towards the jetty. She pulled herself out and hid in the shelter of the trees. It was so dark she couldn't see more than the outline of the leaves. Thankfully her phone still worked and she could find her way through the trees using the torch. The yelling came closer so she turned it off; creeping quietly through the trees.

Alex spotted the path, as she was about to walk out two rangers came running down it with torches. She moved into the rhododendron as they shone the torches through canopy yelling for her to give herself up. Then there was feedback on the radio and they ran off. She waited a minute before taking off down the path in the opposite direction. The map on her phone wasn't loading but there was a sign point to point in the right direction.

There was only one path leading up to the castle. Alex skuttled up the path keeping low. It was dark so she felt her way along not wanting to risk using a light. It took some time but eventually she made it up the battlements.

"Up here," called James's voice softly. Alex looked up and followed his directions. "What took you so long? I was just about to come and find you."

"You're the one who pushed me into the water," Alex retorted, trying to hug him to spread the smell on his horrible dry body. James pushed her away as they bickered for a second until a light from below illuminated the castle. The voices were getting closer so they legged it over the wall and into the woods. James led them through the trees to one of the paths and they ran out of the park. They had emerged on the east side of the park so James hailed a taxi to take them to his apartment. Seeing as he was dry, he gave Alex his coat which she hoped the lake smell would never wash out of.

James had an amazing apartment. It wasn't in one of the rich buildings on fifth avenue but looked out onto the river. It was warm and comfortable. James pointed Alex in the direction of the shower. She handed her clothes out through the door so he could put them on to wash. *I told him to use a whole packet of detergent.* Alex decided to take a bath and had really work the disgusting lake smell out of her hair. James had a hair dryer thankfully but something she noticed the dampeners had broken, leaving her basically naked. She hid them inside her phone case and found a charger. The bathroom had a second door into the bedroom. James had left out some joggers and an NYPD top for her to borrow.

The joggers just sinched in enough for her to keep them on. She had to roll up the hems so that she wouldn't trip. The t-shirt could have been a dress but she tied a knot at the waist. Alex's feet were still a little cold so she rummaged around in his drawers to find a thick pair of socks she could borrow. It was quite a look.

Alex went out into the living room and sat down on the sofa. She couldn't see James anywhere but then some music started. It was slow to start with the beat growing heavier. James turned the lights down before emerging in his police uniform but it was un tucked and messy. He started dancing and thrusting to the beat.

"I know you liked magic mike but what about Juicy James?" He asked, walking over to her, taking off his hat and placing it on her head. Alex let out of a cry of excitement and slight cringe but as the music continued, he got better. It was so hot as he slowly removed his clothes until all he had left on were NYPD boxers, his badge around his neck and sunglasses. She smacked his arse as he started ground against her. James picked Alex up, spinning her around so that she was sitting on his hips as he continued to dance.

James was so close her heart fluttered. She felt the blood rush to her cheeks. The tease and sensations were what made his dance very hot but it came to an end. They lay arm in arm sweating and breathing heavily. The chemistry was nothing she had ever felt before. Alex went in for the next move….

Now the rest is as they say history and private. I spent the night and woke up early. Not on schedule. Eyes off the price

Alex woke up at 5.30 and panicked when she saw the time. She sneaked out of bed finding her clothes and shoes. They were still wet and stinky. She pulled a face as she pushed her feet back into wet shoes, scribbled a good bye note to James, found her phone had died and snuck out. She'd also borrowed twenty dollars out of his wallet with an IOU in the note as her phone couldn't order an uber for herself.

Alex hailed a cab and got serious walk of shame vibes from the taxi driver as he drove her to the west side of the park back to her apartment. To be fair she didn't even have a bra under her rotten clothes. She went up to her apartment, got dressed, replaced the dampeners and abandoned her phone. Alex needed to get another taxi straight out to the door and only got into work only five minutes late. But this was another board meeting.

"Well thank you for joining us this morning miss Alex," Senator announced loudly to the room even though half of the office weren't even there yet.

"I'm sorry I was following up some messages from Captain James office, you know for the case." Alex replied with an emphasis on the name drop. She knew that would shut him up. He looked annoyed and started yelling at the rest of the team for not being on time with his schedule. *God this man was a bastard but I didn't need to work for him for much longer.*

The day dragged on and on. Alex noticed a lot of people in the office were giving her a wide bearing. She must have still smelled a little of the lake. That stench was going to take so long to get rid of. She took her break in union square to get some fresh air. Her eyes were barely staying open at this point and the thought of having a food coma was a little much so Alex went to Starbucks before going back to the office. She decided to use the company card and get a round for everyone.

This way I could subject them all to the smell of the lake just for a few moments and they would have to be nice to get their coffee so it was worth it.

The senator wouldn't let anyone leave until eight in the evening. Alex was not happy with the fourteen-hour days yet the end was in sight. She should have done some work in preparation for the United Nations meeting she was attending very soon. This was important as it was part of the president's plan for Katy.

The president was sending the item she needed via courier but it would be a few days to reach her as it had to be searched, de bugged and then sent on a wild goose trace to ensure that the package wasn't traced back to her apartment. When Alex got home, she collapsed onto the sofa and opened up the encrypted iPad. She had some messages and photos from Rose in their safe house looking happy and loved up. Afterwards she shut her eyes and fell asleep on the sofa and nothing in the world could wake her.

Alex was in such a deep sleep that she didn't hear the noise coming from the floor below. There was a beeping sound. The floor started to get hotter and hotter. She rolled over on the couch and the iPad clattered onto the floor. The noise woke her up and something inside her knew that something was wrong.

The room was getting hazy and her nose stung with the smell of smoke. Alex scooped up the iPad and padded across the floor. The beeping got louder as she opened the door to the balcony and peered over the edge of the railing. There were several fire engines on the ground and people looking up at her. The beeping was the buildings alarm which hadn't been going off in Alex's apartment.

Her heart skipped a beat, as she ran back into the apartment. The door locked behind her. Alex threw open the gun cabinet putting the valuables in there as it was fire proof and pulled out a small kit bag including IDs money, phone, gun and dampeners. The cabinet locked and the casing lined the wardrobe so all her outfits would be safe but it wasn't ventilated so she couldn't hide in there.

Instead, Alex ran for the door to the stairs and felt the heat coming off the handle. Grabbing a rag, she tried the door but it was door locked; the emergency release had been damaged. Her secure apartment was now as secure as a prison. Trying to stay calm she looked round the room for options; the bullet proof glass was too strong to break through and there was no way she could reach the fire escape.

 The lights went out in the flat as the power was cut. Alex pulled out the iPad and pressed the call button. The tech guy answered as she got to my knees as the smoked increased, covering her mouth with the rag.

"Someone's trying to kill me." She gasped down the line spluttering. She needed to get to the balcony as the smoke thickened in the dark.

"I had an alert. Someone is hacking the system. The fire brigade are on their way up to your floor. Just give me a few minutes to stop the hackers." He said down the line with desperation in his voice. Alex crouched and scuttled to the bedroom, grabbing the blanket off the bed and running it under the shower as fast as she could while he typed away. Her eyes were stinging but wrapping herself in the wet blanket shielded her as she crawled out of the bedroom into the living room.

"Go to the balcony and keep your head low. I've got the extraction fan on." He instructed from the iPad. Alex made it to the balcony door sinking to the floor as she tried the handle but this time it wouldn't open. She lay down with her bag slung across her shoulder; grasping the iPad. She laid on the ground on her back trying to get some clean air into her lungs.

"Walter." She croaked as the smoke filtered before coughing again. Her breathe rattled as she drew in nothing to sustain her consciousness.

"Alex just two more seconds I've nearly got it." Walter said, typing hard through the keyboard.

"Walter…"

"That's it. Open the door and climb down the fire escape."

…

"Alex? The door?"

….

"Alex? Dammit come on."

… Clatter. The iPad fell out of her hands.

"All units there is a woman unconscious in the penthouse. Repeat. She is of importance to the beaura. Extract." Walter ordered down the radio. Alex could still hear him but each breathe was painful and it was getting hotter by the second. She lay on the floor her head swimming from her shallow gasps for air.

"Alex come on. Get the door." Walter implored her through gritted teeth. Somehow, she found the strength to roll onto her stomach. The handle was so high. She stretched and her fingers brushed it the first time. That small effort made her head swim with the lack of oxygen. One last effort Alex pulled the handle and the door fell open. There was a buzzing off a helicopter as she crawled and collapsed through the door. She breathed the cold air deeply. There was no feeling like it; the rush of oxygen to her head. The iPad was pinging and Walter was still giving instructions.

"Alex don't talk, stay silent no matter what. I've reset the dampener so you will be disguised. Help is on the way." Were the last words she heard as a helicopter buzzes overhead. A rope fell down to the balcony and someone slid down it. Alex sprawled on her back as the person rushed over and picked her up. They latched a harness around her and attached them to the winch just as an explosion came from the apartment. The person shielded Alex from the heat as the helicopter hoisted them away before the building was consumed in flames. They were winched in, where paramedics were waiting to treat her for smoke inhalation.

The helicopter flew to the nearest hospital as Alex drifted in and out of consciousness; her lungs were on fire. She had a mask over her face as the person who rescued her pulled off his helmet. She must have been delirious as she thought she saw Nicholas's face. But then her eyes rolled up into her head and she blacked out.

***

Alex came round hearing voices around her as her drifted back to the surface of consciousness. Her instincts told her to keep her eyes shut. Each breathe was sore, but it wasn't her body moving of its own accord. Her urge to breathe took over as her lungs inflated on their own; it was an alien and uncomfortable feeling.

Alex flinched; panicking, trying to regain control of her breathing. Her hand shot to her face. Something was covering her eyes. There was a tube down her throat that was making her gag. Her hand was pulled off her face as she twitched and she felt a pain in her arm. A rush of tiredness washed over her as she opened her eyes seeing herself surrounded by doctors looking concerned before the sedative washed over her and she fell back to sleep.

The next time she woke up the pain in her lungs was greatly reduced. Her hand shot up remembering the tube but she only had a mask on and was breathing independently. She opened her eyes to look round the room. It was a private room; her bag was on a chair next to the bed and her iPad was on the bedside table with a video feed.

"Good to see you are awake." said Walter's voice. Alex tried to speak but it takes a couple of attempts as her throat felt like it had been grated.

"What happened?" she finally got out trying to sit up a little.

"The Chinese group that you helped hacked into the system tried to terminate you. They don't know your "real" identity but they got your staff id. Started an electronic fire and disappeared. They had a confirm death before we got to you and they disappeared. Your rescue has been kept off the news and reports. You inhaled a lot of smoke and have been on oxygen for a few days." Walter explained with a tinge of concern in his voice.

"Thank you for getting me out of there." Alex said, sipping some water.

"Sure, but I wasn't the one who rescued you." Walter said, he seemed to be hesitating before he continued.

"You know it's funny, I swear that I remember seeing Nick's face but that must have been a dream." Alex mused leaning back into the pillows feeling a little fragile

"It *was* Nicholas. He was the only one fast enough to respond. But the dampeners were on and he didn't know who you were. I have sent him on a mission to the middle east so that he won't be likely to check up on you while you recover.

"How long have I been asleep?" Alex asked reaching over for the iPad to boot up the internet.

"Just two days until the doctor could get your oxygen levels back up to normal. The smoke that you breathed in had a mild sedative in it which explained how you were so overcome so quickly." Walter informed me. "But Alex you can't go back to the apartment. It has been completely destroyed and we believe it is being monitored." Walter told her looking concerned.

"I figured." Alex said as a coughing fit came over her. When it had subsided, she continued. "This means I have three days until the UN conference. I know I should change identities but this is so important."

"I understand but we have no choice. You have been sacked by Senator Smith for absence. You had missed several days this month and he isn't the most forgiving of bosses. We couldn't alert him that you were ill or dead. You don't need him to get into United Nations conference. You just need to plant the bug on the Russian president. I have a plan to get you in and close to the President." Walter said with firm clear instructions. There must have been some orders from above while she was asleep.

"Walter one problem. If the president uses a dampener won't, he detect my technology and know-how to track me? Or even if it gets discovered by the Russians? There are so many variables that could go wrong." Alex asked concerned, making a pained face as her lungs stung.

"Well, I've been thinking about this and I have come up with a solution." Walter said, pulling out a small case so that it was in view of the iPad camera. "Inside here are tiny electronic barbs. Their so thin that you wouldn't feel them entering your skin. They slide right in between the lines of your finger print. They each have a tiny microchip which attaches onto any Wi-Fi or signal and allows access for monitoring and into the mainframe." Walter explained, carefully showing them to the camera.

"How on earth do they do that?" Alex asked peering at the screen to try and see the barbs.

"It's called nanotech. I will explain it to you one day. These will be waiting for you in your new apartment." He explained putting them away, "Now listen carefully. You need to put the glove on, it will blend straight into your hand and when you go to touch the Russian president take the plastic cover off the glove. Then touch his skin for at least five seconds. These will give the president access to the system in the Russian government. It will match up with the dampener trackers and we can pass the evidence on to the conflicting governments in the future. I will give China access to the threat when the suspicions are raised about the president. It will all be traced back to the influence of the president. Once the barb is in place, you need to leave. Burn the glove as soon as you can. The President will only have so much access to the Russian mainframe and once you have been detected in Moscow he will know that he has been played. All hell is going to break loose." He instructed closing the case as glanced over his shoulder.

"Look I've got to go but I will send these to you. Everything will be waiting for you when you get to your new apartment." Walter said and hung up abruptly as some voices came from behind him. He didn't tell her where the apartment was or what to do next. Alex rested in the bed for the rest of the day until the nurse came in to check on her. She got the all clear to be discharged that evening.

As she prepared to leave a man dressed in black sporting aviators in doors delivered some clothes and essentials, once she was dressed escorting her to the new apartment. The dampeners were still working despite the smoke damage and extended usage. They drove up the east side of the park and pulled up outside the dingiest looking building on the upper east side.

The escort assisted her out of the car, handed her bag with a set of keys and then drove off. Alex walked in dilapidated entrance finding that there wasn't a lift. The note on the side of the key read 6. She started to take the stairs very slowly as her lungs stung with the effort.

Eventually, Alex got herself to the top floor she found that there was only one door on the landing. She was a little breathless on the way up but eagerly put the key in to the lock and the door swung open. She blinked a few times as she looked into the most beautiful apartment she had ever seen.

It was magnificent with a full console and hacking system, exquisite furniture and a skylight which filled the space with natural light. She shut the door behind her, turning the manual lock. A new phone was waiting for her on the kitchen bench. She turned it on as she checked out the fully stocked fridge. There was a remote control which changed the temperature, fire, tv and the lights which she didn't explore as the phone started vibrating excessively. The phone was fully loaded with her contacts and messages.

Alex settled on the corner sofa and scrolled through the emails. She had a notice of contract termination from Senator Smiths office and deleted it without a second thought. To the Chinese clients wouldn't suspect anything she would need to keep out of the limelight. There were messages from her colleagues and more media messages. Everything needed to be deleted as if she had never existed but one element was going to be hard to ignore.

There was several missed calls and texts from James. The messages brought tears to her eyes. He was close to starting a man hunt for her after seeing the explosion in his reports and no trace of her in any local hospital. This had to be shut down in person. Alex pressed the call button on her phone and James answered on the second ring.

"Alex? Is that you?" He asked. His voice didn't sound right.

"Yes," she paused to cough "It's me. Sorry I haven't called I just got my phone back."

"Where have you been?" He asked sounding very anxious

"I was in hospital for smoke inhalation." Alex replied. The effort of speaking was a lot so she went through to the kitchen to get some water. He heard her discomfort over the phone.

"I've been beside myself. I saw the report the next day about the fire. There was no record of anyone being hurt and everyone was accounted for but I couldn't get hold of you I thought you had been burnt to a crisp." James explained, his voice shook as he said it, pulling at Alex's heart strings.

"I'm sorry." She paused to take a deep breathe feeling her eyes water. "I woke up in hospital and I had to be on oxygen for a few hours and then they released me. You know what they can be like once they can't get hold of your insurance." Alex tried to explain but it seems to make him more adjugated.

"You have insurance, don't you?" James asked sounding shocked.

"Of course, I do. They put me on emergency support and I was able to give them the information afterwards." Alex explained, trying to calm him down a little. She took a moment to take a couple of deep breathes before continuing the conversation.

"Your apartment has burnt down. Come and stay with me. I will pick you up." He said and she could hear him get up for his keys. "No, I'm ok, I'm staying with my cousin in the city." Alex replied quickly putting her cup of water down on the table and putting her head in her hand. "I just want to sleep tonight and take tomorrow as it comes." Alex just had to buy herself a few days to finish the next phase of the mission, then she could sort all of this out. James wouldn't let up.

"Let me take you out to dinner tomorrow. My treat, just to make sure that you are ok." He insisted.

*Typical, we find a perfect gentleman who always shows up when needed and I can't do anything to encourage him. *

Now I know you've been watching Disney! We don't need to rely on anyone. Stop looking for someone to rescue us. Shut it down and watch true crime instead; something that might be useful.

No, it's my turn to be in control

"Fine, take me to dinner tomorrow tonight. Now you need to let me sleep," Alex replied bluntly, hanging up with phone. About thirty seconds later, she got a text saying that they had reservations at a small restaurant in Soho for the next day. Alex texted James her new address so that he could pick her up. She went to explore the rest of the apartment.

The bedroom was hidden behind some teak sliding doors. It didn't have a view yet the sky light extended into the bedroom. The lights came on as she entered to see the basic layout. She opened the door to the walk-in wardrobe to find a full ammunition and tech set up hidden with a letter waiting for her in Walters hand writing. Alex pulled letter open and started reading the instructions. It was going to be a complex plan with some intricate preparation.

I won't reveal the details as it will ruin what happened next.

Eventually, she fell asleep on top of the bed since she was so exhausted. Alex woke up in the middle of the night. The lights had dimmed; she could see the stars shining through the skylight. The room had a little bit of a chill so she buried herself under the covers; lying flat on her back was still a little laboured. Alex stacked the pillows so that she was lying at forty-five degrees and drifted back off again.

The next day she slept in. It was the first time Alex didn't need to be up in weeks and she decided to make the most of it. James was picking her up at seven which gave her the whole day to prepare. *Basically, a kept woman.*

In the meantime, it would be good to do some mission preparation. The UN building had a high security system but there was a server's entrance. She used some of the skills which Walter had taught her so long ago, printed off some IDs and peeled them onto plastic fobs. Alex recharged the dampeners; loaded all the faces she would need to enter the building. She would need to do a few outfit and wig changes on top of the face IDs. The glove was going to be at the last minute. It would be concealed on my person throughout the deploy.

Once Alex got into the conference, she needed to work out who she would be so that she was able to make contact with the Russian president. What members of staff would be able to contact him? She scrolled through the president's mainframe on the iPad. None of the staff and tasks that would deem them safe enough to meet with the foreign presidents. Until one face appeared on the screen. Miss Erin Defraz newly promoted manager of the president's media team giving briefs and liaising with interviewees. She had emails from every press office from the countries that were attending the summit. This was going to be her ticket once she was in the building. Walter had already worked out the logistics to the plan which she could study.

When she was finished, Alex closed the laptop after sending the information to Walter to start making security passes and programming the dampeners which was going to take a day at least. Bed was the most appealing option right now despite her long lie. She glanced at the clock and noticed it was nearly 3pm. Her new bed was so comfortable. It took her a while to get sleep. Alex felt safer sleeping with the light on but then woke up abruptly a few hours later feeling like she was suffocating having rolled onto her side.

The clock said it was six. Alex had an hour so she went into the bathroom and stared at the mess looking back at her in the mirror. She had some serious bed head, massive blue bags under her eyes and there was a little of bit of an odour in the air.

After a long shower she looked semi decent, checking the clock she was running late. She blasted her hair with the hair dryer and put it up in a pony tail, pulled on some smart clothes and put her spare dampeners on which saved a lot of time.

Instead of putting on heels she grabbed some ankle boots out of the cupboard and hurried down the stairs as fast as she could. When she reached the bottom of the stairs her dampeners started vibrating. The notification pinged on her phone and smart watch that they had low battery.

After a fair amount of swearing and running back up the stairs to grab the fully charged one. She made it down to the front of the building where James was waiting for her. He didn't give her any hint to where they were going. He held her hand the whole journey as if he wasn't sure if she was there. The stress had taken its toll on him over the past few days but he kept smiling for her. They drove down the Times Square and got out on 42nd street which had been her favourite haunt when she was hiding in New York

"Oh my gosh you are taking me to see Phantom?" Alex burst out as they got out in the street, squeaking with glee and bouncing on the balls of her feet. She had resisted coming to see it in so long but if she hadn't bought the tickets what could be the harm in going to see the show.

"Em, no we are going to see Frozen," he paused concerned and turned Alex around to face the opposite direction. The frozen musical was Phantom's neighbour which she had never seen it as it wasn't in New York when she had spent all her time at the shows. "Are you disappointed?" He asked sounding anxious. She gasped with excitement that he had planned her perfect date.

"No, oh my god this is amazing!" Alex said gleefully and punched him hard on the shoulder with excitement. A little harder than she meant to but he laughed off the gesture.

"If I had known you were such a musical fan, I would have taken you to see something a lot sooner than this." James said happily as Alex dragged him across the road to stand in line for the doors. The crowd started to form outside the doors but James pushed ahead and flashed his badge at the door. They were let in early which made Alex at the annoyed faces around them. Ironically it was very cold today so the rest of the audience had to wait outside in the nasty weather.

They didn't go straight into the show instead got drinks at the expensive bar. Alex nipped to the bathroom while there wasn't going to be a queue. James had a bottle of champagne waiting for them when she got back. The stage manager came out to greet them as Alex popped the cork. James shook his hand and introduced her. The manager's wife was a detective on the force who knew James and had sorted them out with tickets. He advised her that we had the best seats in the house. This former stage manager was going to be the judge of that.

After about twenty minutes, they let the rest of the crowd in and they made our way to their seats. Alex was shocked when they were led up the side thinking we were in a box but they had incredible seats in the royal circle. They were right in the centre at the balcony. These might have been the most expensive seats as allowed had the widest view of the stage. Alex was seriously impressed.

I won't tell you about what happens in the show in case one day you decide to go and see it. There was so much going on and so many clever visual effects. I was so impressed as an ex-manager. Although I would never have been able to say any of this to James.

The show finished; Alex was the first audience member up to give a standing ovation trying to hide the tears from her eyes. She was joined by James who let out an incredible whistle. The theatre emptied which made Alex wanted to rush out to go and meet the cast outside. *One of the actors was shredded.* But James waited behind for a second and refusing to let her meet him.

"What's wrong?" she asked and pulled on his hand. He kept his face away from hers, whipped his eyes away with his sleeve. "Are you crying?" Alex asked reaching up to pull his face towards hers.

"No," He said quickly, "Oh look," he squawked, coughed to clear his throat and in a deeper than usual voice, "the stage manager is waving at us again. Better go see what she wants." James said and took the stairs two at a time to go see his friend; leaving Alex in a hysterical giggling fit. She collected their glasses to drop them at the bar at the top of the house while following James with his coat. The looks from the staff told her that no one ever offered to clean up after themselves.

"Oh, that's very kind of you to help out Miss," said the stage manager taking the items off me and giving them to a member of staff who was passing by with a bin bag. She seemed shocked that Alex even had touched the glasses.

"I don't mind I used to wait tables." Alex explained, smiling at the cleaner as they hurried away. The waiter smiled behind the managers back, disappearing into the corridor.

"There are a few customers meeting the cast in costume tonight before we close up. Do you want to join them?" James asked her. He put an arm round her waist because she looked like she could pass out from excitement. The smoke inhalation still made her feel light headed with too much excursion.

"Does a three-legged dog swim in a circle?" she asked, the stage manager laughed and lead them back down to the foyer where around a dozen of other customers were waiting; Elsa, Christoff, Olaf puppet and grand Pappay. Alex spent a while talking with Elsa and asking lots of questions about the special effects and costumes. Elsa was impressed with her knowledge and was too happy to oblige. Alex resisted taking a photo with her just in case but it was incredible. James watched on happily while chatting with his friend until she reached the last character.

Grand Pappay was the last person left to talk to. He wasn't portrayed as old. He was ripped and only wearing trousers with a tail. Alex was pretty much eye level with his abs. He was making her laugh and there was a touch of flirting happening between them. *To be honest I can't remember I was very starstruck but with that torso who couldn't help but drool.* James appeared at her side and shook hands very firmly with the actor nearly glowering at him and marking his territory. This was all too funny; she had never seen him display any kind of jealous behaviour. All too soon, it was time to leave. They thanked the stage manager and James lead her outside. Both of them were starving but it was quite late so a lot of places would be shut.

"Where do you want to go to eat. I know a fancy sushi place up the road that we could go to." Suggested James looking at his watch.

"Can I take you somewhere?" Alex asked and James seemed keen on the idea. She got the map up on her phone, leading him down a few streets until we got to one of the oldest diners in New York. There weren't many left as they would often run out of business and be replaced with a chain store like Starbucks or McDonalds. Alex had wanted to go here for so long and it was protected. It was styled like it had been in the fifties with every inch of wall space covered in signs and pictures. Plus, they did twenty-four-hour food.

It wasn't on one of the nicer areas of town but it was low key and friendly which was exactly what she wanted. It just felt more like something Alex would go for back in London. A happy little place that wasn't well known yet still loved by those who knew about it. They sat down and ordered the biggest burgers on the menu. James looked sceptically at them when they arrived.

"Are you sure this is real meat?" he asked removing the top of the bun and examining the contents.

"Who cares," Alex rolled her eyes, taking a massive bite out of hers. The sauce seeped everywhere, all over her face and hands. The burger disintegrated on to the table. She started laughing with her mouth full at James's expression of horror to the point she started choking. He thumped her hard on the back and Alex managed to swallow her gob full but the sauce made her look deranged. She kept going with her disintegrated burger and encouraged James to try his.

"You know I would never do this on a first date." Alex admitted trying to wipe some of the mess off her face.

"I don't think it's doing you any favours on this one either." James remarked back. He had been threatening to take a picture of the mess and making it his wallpaper. Though he had been enjoying his own burger and only left the chips. Alex left him too got to the bathroom to clean herself up a little as James went to change the music on the duke box. She ran the water at full blast and splashed in on her face to wash off the sauce. When she was finished, Alex turned the tap off; instead of music there was yelling coming from the main diner.

Alex snuck back down the corridor to find everyone on the floor. She was confused if it was a dance move then looking round to see men in masks with guns. They were robbing the till. One of the men spotted her peering round the corner.

"Put your hands up!" yelled one of them in a balaclava. Alex did as she was told as he approached her. She took a deep breathe to compose herself; running through her training in her mind. In one swift move disarmed him, knocked him to the ground and pointed the gun at him as he lay on the floor.

"Why don't you put your hands up!" Alex suggested to the other robber. Alex looked around for James who is looking directly at her opening his mouth to yell a warning as another man grabbed her from behind. He pulled a beefy arm around her neck, knocking the gun out of her hand. It clattered to the floor. Alex kicked it across the room to James. There was a third man emptying the register. The first needed a moment to regain his dignity getting up from the ground.

"Don't try to be smart again will you sweetheart." He glowered at her; Alex booted him straight in the face with her heel breaking his nose.

"NYPD FREEZE," James yelled getting to his feet, raising the weapon and pointed it straight into the first man's back.

"Alright cop. We're going to do this nice and easy. You let us got and everyone in here lives. Including your girlfriend." He growled into Alex's hair. She shifted hard in his arms but he tightened his grip around her neck making her head spin again as the adrenaline spiked. "Sound like a fair deal?" The third man said, backing away to the door, pulling Alex with him. James stood ready as the third stepped outside followed by the other two. Alex was the only thing keeping James from shooting the man who kept a very tight grip on her throat. They backed out of the diner door.

"I will let her go outside. Stay put and give us a head start." The man ordered; James nodded reaching for his phone. The man hauled Alex out. There was no getaway car, the other two robbers were fleeing down the street. When they reached the pavement Alex managed to get her hand under the man's elbow.

"Sweetheart, time to make our fair wells." He said into her ear knowing that James would be there any second.

"True, but say hi to your jail mates for me." Alex replied pulling her arm through his headlock, breaking free and twisting his arm behind his back; with one strong kick to the shoulder his arm came out of its socket. He let out the most girlish of screams.

"Enjoy prison sweet heart." Alex laughed and kick him between the legs as James emerged from the diner, on the phone. His gun was raised. He stopped in shock, staring at the man on the floor with Alex standing over him. "Get him cuffed, I'll get the others." she instructed excitedly choosing not to hear James's yells as she took off after the other two thieves. The adrenaline pumping through her forgetting the pain in her lungs. Alex knew all her running and personal training was going to pay off at some point.

She tore after the other two men, making up the ground easily. They had stopped in a nearby alley to count the money and wait for their friend to arrive. The sirens screaming down the road as Alex approached them in the alley. She smiled mischievously.

"Do you guys want to give the money back?" Alex asked with her hands on her hips. The man she had accosted in the diner legged it away, his nose still bleeding. Alex snatched the bag out of the third man's hands who turned and ran after his friend. They were fast but so was she. She flung the money bag into a dumpster; taking chase, dodging between the cars and pedestrians. The man jumped on top of a dumpster and leapt for the ladder to a fire escape.

Before he could climb up the ladder, Alex leapt after him, using her full body weight to pull him down. They both fell together. It was only about twelve feet; Alex's fall was cushioned by the robber. There was a crack as his ankle broke as they hit the ground. She pinned him down, he wasn't going anywhere.

"Hand's up!" yelled his friend in front of her with his gun raised. Alex felt the blood surge through her veins as she stared down the barrel. A smirk emerged on his face as she raised her hands. The sound of the gun went off causing her to flinch. The man holding the gun fell to the ground with a bullet in his shin. Alex saw James at the entrance to the alley, he was breathing heavily as he lowered the gun. The relief coursed through her as she held down the one with the broken ankle.

James cuffed the two men as the police caught up with them. Alex was panting with the effort of holding the second perp as her adrenaline spike dropped finally. Her heart rate was slowing and she could feel the bruises across her body and scrapes on her arms and legs. Her lungs were on fire.

"You are crazy!" James said. "Totally crazy. What in god's name were you doing chasing after gun men." He asked, looking like he wanted to shake her. She could hear the awe in his voice but he was furious at the same time.

"Oh, come on these idiots?" Alex laughed, shaking the whole thing off. "I'm surprised you didn't step in earlier; not that I need a guy to defend me. Anyway, they were robbing the diner, I had to do something." Alex replied happily but she could tell it was coming across as reckless.

"Where is the money?" James asked as the men were taken away.

"Oh yeah I stashed it," Alex remembered and jogged back across the road to the dumpster she had thrown the bag into. Without a moment's hesitation she jumped right in, rummaged through the rubbish until she found the right back and jumped out. "Here it is," Alex handed the bag to the officer waiting with

James. They both looked at each other as if she was off her rocker.

"Let's get you back to my place where you can at least have a shower. I might need to do a summary of what happened with you." James suggested, handing the money over to his colleague.

"Sure," Alex replied, realising how badly she smelled. Maybe jumping in the dumpster wasn't the best idea in the world. James ordered them an uber to drive up town and the man asked if she would sit on a towel. They got to James's apartment, before she could enter, he blocked her way.

"Where do you think you're going in those disgusting clothes!" He said, pulling her in a fireman's lift so she wouldn't touch the carpet. He shoved her in the shower fully clothed, removed the hose and sprayed her from head to toe with Alex screaming in protest until the water heated up. Once he was satisfied, he left a big towel on the heater and took her clothes to wash along with his.

I know we had been in this situation once before but the only similarity was that lake and dumpsters smell equally as bad as each other!

Alex stole his dressing gown and put her hair up to join him on the sofa. James gave Alex a good sniff before he let her sit with him. They curled up all warm and cosy.

"You are one crazy girl." James repeated putting his arms around her. "You've saved me from the gunmen, you've stopped three thieves. Tell me is your real identity superwoman?" He asked which made her laughed in response.

"No, I just workout and have a background in martial arts. Anyway, you helped. You stopped the third one so I might give you fifteen percent of the credit." Alex replied which she considered to be generous.

"Please promise me that we will have a date where I won't be at risk of losing my badge for once?" James asked, with a snort.

"We could count the date as when frozen finished and, in that way, we have a success rate of safe dates as one and it can only go up from there. Or we could go to an art gallery to stop a heist?" Alex suggested, she could find some crime for them to stop on her iPad with a little bit of hacking.

"Or down." He counter offered. His arms tightened ever so slightly, giving her the impression that he thought she might go out again. "You are the most independent woman I have ever met. My whole life I've had to protect everyone; my family, the people of New York. You just take everything as it comes and kick it in the face apparently." He observed thoughtfully, stroking her arm with his thumb.

Now we seem to be his therapist for superhero syndrome. Maybe I can get on board with this guy if he stops being so cheesy...

*Don't ruin the moment! *

I'm not I'm saying he might be acceptable for us now.

*Aww is that you starting to open up to the prospect of love? *

That is NOT what I am saying.

I knew you liked it when we watched Bridget Jones

Why don't you listen and reply to him rather than argue with yourself?

"Well, I wasn't always like that. I learned to be independent. There is no point waiting around for the world to serve you everything on a silver platter. You need to be prepared for anything and not willing to accept personal gains through items or ambition. It's a very positive mindset to live in." Alex replied thoughtfully to James as he took in her reply.

"I think the reason I rose through the police ranks was so that I could make the biggest difference as a captain. But you have shown me that maybe I didn't need to do it that way." James said, making Alex twist in his arms to look at him. He stroked the side of her face with his finger.

"You can make an amazing difference as a police captain. Ways you probably haven't even thought of. People look up to you, you are like a guiding light for those stuck in the dark." Alex smiled sweetly at him as he started playing with her hair.

"Well, if I'm the light then you are my electricity." He said and leaned down to kiss her. Alex lifted her head to meet his but a beep from her phone brought her back to reality. The united nation summit was tomorrow. *Oh shite, the mission.* Without an explanation, she leapt out of his lap like a spring and ran to grab some clothes.

"You also have the worst attention span I think I have ever experienced," he said with a sigh. James seemed to notice a pattern of behaviour with Alex. Mostly her disappearing.

"I'm sorry I need to go. I have to water the plants in my apartment." Alex replied pulling on random garments in the hall.

"What are you on about and can I get my hoodie back this time?" James asked as she hurried out the door pulling on her shoes.

"You want it, you're going to have to come find it!" Alex yelled taking the stairs two it a time and leaping the last ones onto the foyer floor. She was in a taxi when she scrolled through her phone to the angry messages from Walter. A message from James pinged up.

"Don't stop any bank robberies or jewellery heists without me x"

All or Nothing

Alex walked up to the United Nations building wearing janitors' overalls and scanned her ID round the back entrance to the building. The security was crazy at the front however in the service entrance she was only patted down and had the metal detector run over. There were numerous journalists scattered through the building waiting the announcement of the climate change agreement. Alex could look them in the eye knowing that at some point her name would have been reported but they would never know. It was expected that the American president was going create a lot of conflict in the deal as he didn't personally believe in climate change. Alex was watching for the president's media assistant; Erin DeFraz.

Alex still had a trace on her from the dampener she hid on her in China. Walter did something very clever; her dampener was able to triangulate her radio and Wi-Fi signal from her phone giving Alex not only a precise location but her elevation too. She had been very helpful spreading decoy dampeners signals around the world which they would use at another time. Walter caused all the cameras to loop as Alex passed so there would be no record of her being in the building.

When Erin was located Alex followed her into the bathroom; locking the door behind her and pressed a button on her phone. A short electric burst flowed out of the dampener stunning Erin. This gave Alex a second to inject her with a sedative and hid her into the supply closet.

Erin was asleep within seconds. Alex took her blouse and earpiece out and locked the cupboard behind her. She would be back to wake her in a few minutes. They had timed it all perfectly. The voice on the ear piece was sending out instructions to get the leaders together for the group picture.

Alex had to go and brief the leaders of where to sit; the president wanted to be featured front and central. The amount of instructions Erin was given was ridiculous. She had to be fast. Alex's heart pounded as she entered the room with the world representatives.

Once she was in the hall she pulled on the glove and exposed the barbs on her finger, this was the only chance she would get to be close to the Russian president. Alex walked up to the American president but before she could show him to his seat, he pulled her aside cause Alex to momentarily panic that he recognised her.

"I don't want to be sat next to the Russian president." He breathed down her neck. Alex looked up at him but didn't say anything for a moment; praying that the voice chip would activate. It had been recording Erin for the last week, downloading into the chip in her neck and would change Alex's voice as she spoke. "Put me next to the British prime minister instead." The American President ordered her. Keeping her face calm, Alex braved her voice chip.

"Think of the publicity if you are shoulder to shoulder on the climate change with the leading opposition on the climate change bill. The newspapers will lap it up." Alex tried to convince him otherwise, it was vital that he sat next to him.

"I assume this will benefit me in the re-election next year." The president replied thoughtfully too which Alex nodded but did not look happy by the fact. "Also has there been any issues with security?" The president asked in a more conserved voice. Her heart nearly dropped to the floor; did he know?

"No sir, the security council have taken every measure necessary." Alex replied a little too fast. He looked quite annoyed. The president grumbled inaudibly under his breathe, his eyes scanning the room as he stalked over to the seats. Alex followed him and gestured to the specific seat he needed as they were joined by the Russian president and his aide.

"Sir," Alex said boldly to the Russian as he turned round to look at her. "My name is Erin Defraz," she said holding out her hand to him with baited breath. For a second, Alex didn't think he was going to take my hand but he reached out and accepted her hand. She held on counting the Mississippi's in her head. He hand didn't flinch as the needles slide in and she let go of his hand as he scowled at her. Alex introduced him to the American president who shook hands politely before the pair turned to pose for the camera. Her heart hammered as she dismissed herself for the photos to be taken. She tried not to sag with relief. It was done.

The closet remained locked so Alex slipped in and administer the drug to wake Erin up, replace her shirt; resetting her own dampeners and voice chip. Erin started to rouse as Alex guided her out into the hall supporting her weight.

"Are you ok, you looked like you were about to faint?" Alex gaslit her, keeping her arm around Erin's waist as the drugs wore off.

"Oh, I'm not sure, "she said groggily. "Oh yes, I did feel weird." The sedative wore off as quickly as it had knocked her out. Alex had replaced the ear piece so she could hear the instructions filtering through. Alex also removed the dampener from her neck. Poor Erin had served her purpose and if something happened, she wouldn't want her associated with the Cover Girl by carrying any tech. Erin stood up properly; rushing over to the door back into the main wing as if nothing had happened.

"Are you sure that you are, ok?" Alex asked again but Erin paused at the door still looking confused. She shook her head a disappeared and that was Alex's que to go too. She passed straight into the swarm of the media waiting in and outside the building. Amongst the sea of photographers and reporters. She swapped her clothes, reset the dampeners and vanished into the crowd; getting into an uber at a safe distance and throwing the phone out the window.

The next phase of the operation was simply lie low and wait for the president to get in contact with the Cover Girl. He was going to need her desperately with China in his mainframe and the evidence of his influence in Russia being tracked by the media. *I wonder who tipped them off?*

Now the ball was in Katy's court; she was going to disappear. A week passed and Alex spent the time alone in her apartment which was SO boring. She couldn't even go to visit James. She tried yoga, subscription services on the massive wide screen in the lounge. At the point she was considering *cleaning* for entertainment; a call from Walter came on the iPad.

"It's time." Walter said through the mic, typing crazily on his computer. "Remember the call is being tracked by the pentagon and I can only keep you hidden if the call is no more than three minutes long so put the stop watch on your phone. Any longer and they will trace the decoy back within their system which will compromise me and leave you on your own!" He instructed giving her the signal to give him thirty seconds before she answered. With a deep breathe to prepare herself and turn on the voice chip, Alex answered the call.

"Hello Miss Jones this is the president." Came the voice through the iPad.

"Good evening, Sir," Alex replied politely.

"I would like to confirm that contract has been completed in full. My clients have access to the mainframe. I was not sure if you had kept to the contract but I am impressed with your work. I wanted to personally thank you for your efforts and professionalism. I assumed as I didn't see you that you hadn't fulfilled it." He said coolly through the microphone.

"Thank you, I assumed the confidentiality clause is going to be adhered to in our contract." Alex replied trying to keep the conversation brief.

"I can assure you that you will never hear from me again." The president replied reassuringly. "Payment has been made in full. Don't spend it too fast. Sums like this are hard to declare." Alex's heart started beating as she watched the timer run down.

"Thank you, sir, but I am going to need to terminate this call as I am actually working tonight. Good luck with the rest of your term." She replied in a mild panic end the connection before he could reply with a sigh of relief.

"Well done." Walter exclaimed through the iPad. "Now we just need to sit back and wait for him to slip up before we move to phase three of the plans."

"Oh yes. Please remind me of what I need to do again." Alex replied almost giddy with relief and sprawl over the sofa in excitement.

"You need to go out into the world and make yourself known again. Be seen in the back of pictures and use transactions in your name. No pattern just random places you fancy. You need to officially come out of hiding." Walter instructed which made Alex scream with joy. Walter covered his ears down the mic.

Land of the Free

One week later

Katy was finally free. She needed to make the president think that he had been scammed and her first location was going to be St Petersburg to visit the winter palace after a visit to the local mafia. She had flights booked the very next morning. She had used her own name and gone on a very expensive shopping spree around the city; creating traceable transactions.

Oh, I could just think of the president's face when he realised that the Cover Girl had been working within Russia.

After that Alex wasn't sure where she was going to go. However, she needed to keep returning to New York as there was someone else's attention she needed to attract. According to Walter, Nicholas was back in the city from his mission deployment. The president wanted her in as soon as her booking to Russia had gone through.

Every way to communicate with her had been blocked and all the money had been transferred out of the original account. She was a ghost in the wind taunting him. The President though she was a fake agent of Russia and evidence of China hacking their system had been traced back to a woman called the Cover Girl. All the bread crumbs that had been left were finally being picked up. There was a mission to bring her in within the FBI itself. The truth would reveal itself in the end.

Dear god how have they not worked it out already?

Alex needed to make Nicholas think that he had seen her. Take the bait so that he would follow the path she had laid out for him over all of those months. He was set up with a flat in lower Manhattan. He was working for the FBI and working his way up quickly through the ranks. Walter was one of his best friends and they saw each other almost every time he had been in the city. Alex was so close to potentially getting her life back the prospect was exciting.

Alex packed a bag that night to make her way to the airport. She had booked herself a first-class ticket landing in Moscow. A private car picking her up taking her to the Hilton hotel. The next morning, she was picked up by her new security team; one was called Igor and the other Sergei. Alex had ordered a full new designer outfit to be waiting for her in Moscow. *I can't tell you how good it felt to be back in Chanel.* The escorts were polite, sitting in stony silence the whole journey. Alex was asked to avert her eyes as they turned down some side streets.

The car pulled up next to a large derelict building; it looked like an office block but on the inside, it was something much grander. Alex was taken into meeting space; she sat down in front of the main desk with Igor and Sergei flanking her side facing a mafia boss with three times the number of people. She could tell that everyone was armed to the teeth despite this being a friendly meeting.

One of the boss's men offered her a vodka drink. She accepted to be polite although she dared not drink anything. The objective today was to seem interested in a partnership; yet not take on any contracts. Her face was on camera, the one that the president had met in the bunker as Rose, that was all that mattered. The mafia men would never recognise her again on the street.

At the end of the meeting, Alex thanked them, leaving without striking a deal. They wanted to make a play on the black market and use her as a connection to the different mafias around the world. As she hadn't learnt anything that would ever be useful in that area of crime. The American intelligence would know nothing about the proposal so their minds would soar to the worst possibilities.

 Alex was escorted back to car and driven back to the hotel by Sergei and Igor. They didn't say a word the whole trip. She entered, got changed in the bathroom and left straight through the back entrance as a member of staff. This might have been a good time to head straight back to the airport but she had a different idea in mind.

Alex got on a train and rode it to St Petersburg. Any nineties kid would appreciate the beauty of the film Anastasia. She wasn't going to miss a chance to go to see the winter palace. *Yes, this was a little bit of an Alex patterned behaviour but after all she was trying to be seen in as many places as possible. Make predictable moves so Nicholas would know that it was her.*

The train took the night to arrive in St Petersburg giving Alex the day to go exploring in the city. The palace was as beautiful as she had imagined it. She had the audio guide as she explored the palace; when she entered the ball room Alex put on the Anastasia soundtrack in her air pods to live the film and what she imagined it would be like to be a Russian grand duchess.

Alex didn't want to leave but her flight back to New York was in a few hours. She flew first class again however; she was so tired she didn't get to enjoy the luxuries. She landed in the wee hours of the morning which was the opportune time to sneak back into the city. There were a few days to kill before her next trip. She entertained herself on her phone on the long journey back to her apartment. The driver was taking a detour so as to charge her extra money. Next time she was just going to get the train from the airport. There were a lot of missed calls from James and from his WhatsApp he was online.

"Hello," James answered immediately.

"Hey you, sorry I've missed your calls I have just been crazy busy job hunting." Alex lied through her teeth.

"It's ok I'm *used* to you appearing and disappearing." James replied a little bluntly. He sounded like he was in the middle of something important.

"Do you want to meet up tonight?" she asked him hopefully.

"I'm sorry I can't tonight. There is a really important case that I'm working on and it might be an all-nighter," he said apologetically.

"Oh, ok," Alex said trying to hide her disappointment. Damn now she knew how he felt when she flitted in and out of his life

"I'm sorry you know I would much prefer to spend time with you." He said down the phone sounding pretty guilty. The warmth returned to his voice. He was genuinely stressed and not mad at her.

"No listen it's fine. I will just entertain herself with a movie night." Alex replied sympathetically. "Call me when you are finished. I'll be waiting." She hung up the phone and sigh. It took another hour to even get back into the city and then it was the middle of the morning and the traffic was grid lock. She went to the apartment to dump her bag. After so many months of nights in, Alex was sick of it and had to get herself seen around the city. What would be something very Alex or Katy to do?

She opened her tablet and research the shows that were on Broadway. There were a few that caught her attention but nothing really to get her to go to a matinee and the last-minute seats would probably be rubbish. Alex did fancy doing something with a little bit of alcohol and a beat. Netflix was on the screen and the advertisement for RuPaul's drag race came on as a new series had been released.

Something that I have to admit is that I have become obsessed with RuPaul over the last few months. I watched all twelve seasons and all-stars back-to-back and so many of the queens talked about the New York drag scene being one of the best in the world.

After a little googling, Alex found that the best drag bars were in Greenwich village. She put on something sparkly with a pair of big shoes and booked the uber to come to pick her up in the evening.

All she could remember from the night was meeting some of the mostly shady, beautiful bitches ever. The queens did a mix of stand up, cabaret and lip singing. The atmosphere was like nothing else and Alex was accepted into the crowd within minutes. She vaguely remembered buying everyone in the bar around of tequila; singing on top of the bar to Katy Perry with one of the queens and dancing off with one of the acts. That is as much as she could remember but when the bar closed, Alex joined her new friends to an invited to an after party.

First thing was first they did was to dress her up a bit. Alex the dampeners off in the low light of the club loo. One of them got an incredible dress which hugged every inch and curve. The queens normally shaped themselves to fit into the dress but this one fit her like a glove. The night had a lot of alcohol and dancing.

The after-party venue closed at 5am; Alex assured the queens she could get home safely. She ordered an uber which pulled up and refused to take her as she was way too drunk. The queens offered Alex a placed to crash. She politely refused deciding to take the subway instead.

Despite the stickiness of the subway floor, Alex walked barefoot as she scrolled through her phone on the way to the train. She pressed redial on the last call. On the tenth ring James answered.

"JAMES," Alex exclaimed loudly. "Did you swoop in a save Manhattan?" She asked staggering down the subway steps.

"No, I only got in an hour ago. My lieutenant took over the case. Are you ok?" He replied sounding concerned.

"I'm goo…" She hiccups mid-sentence. "Good, I'm just walking to the subway but I'm a little tired so I'm going to sit down."

"What, no go get a cab home. I will pay." He said sounding anxious. "Where are you?" Alex let out an exasperated sigh, rolling her whole head instead of her eyes. She reached the line she thought was correct and sank to the floor in the middle of the empty platform

"Nah they wouldn't take me." She replied with a big yawn down the phone, letting her eyes rest for a moment.

"Where are you?" James demanded, making clattering noises as he rushed out of the apartment. Alex's grip started to slacken. "Don't fall asleep!"

"I'm in the village I think." Alex sighed and took a picture of the platform to send to him. She leant her head down against the floor. The station retained the heat from the trains making it stiflingly hot. She just needed to sit here there to get her energy back. Alcohol and jet lag didn't mix.

"There's a taxi rank near you, if I send you directions, I can organise a lift home for you." James suggested through the phone. "Hello?" Alex let out a snore in reply and the phone slipped out of her hand but the video was enabled. "For god's sake, stay there," James ordered. He could only see her face plastered against the floor, drooling on the concrete. He remained on the phone the whole time talking to her as he rushed to get a taxi. Next thing she found someone shaking her gently against the suddenly rough concrete.

"Alex, time to get up. Wow that make up." James's voice was next to her. "Can you get up so we can go home?" he asked. Alex shook her head. Everything was spinning, she felt arms underneath her carrying her off the platform. Alex didn't remember the rest of the night as she passed out again. She woke up in a large bed with a fluffy duvet draped over her. The light was blinding and her head throbbed like a hammer was striking it.

Alex groaned, got up to go to the bathroom and let out a shriek as she saw the drag make up caked over her face. It was a bold look; the cat eyes as big as her lid and extreme contour. She started laughing hard as James ran to the bathroom.

"Are you ok?" he gasped looking like he had hardly slept a wink.

"Yes, I just got a bit of a shock when I looked in the mirror," Alex replied as she started scrubbing the make-up off with the running water.

"I'm not surprised you look like the joker!" James said giving her a weary smile. Alex looked anxiously at him.

"Why are you so tired? We didn't do anything last night did we?" she asked running through the course of the night in her mind in a mild panic.

"No don't worry. With that face nothing was going to happen, I would be too scared. I crashed on the sofa to give you space and that face was going to give me nightmares." He said, swiftly dodging a boot on the bum from her.

"Well, my friends wanted to give me a makeover and apparently I will say yes to anything after a few drinks." Alex looked up at him making him snort with laugher at the extreme panda eyes she had remaining. He wouldn't have any make up remover.

"Oh, I already knew that." James said with a hint of a grin on his face. His eyes wandered as Alex noticed for the first time she was just in her underwear.

"Where are my clothes?" Alex asked putting her hands on her hips and raising her eye brows at him.

"Hey I put you to bed fully clothed but what you did afterwards is on you. I tidied up after you though so they are here." James said opening up the cupboard. Alex held up the dress realising that she could not go out in public wearing it. Instead, she riffled through James's sports drawer to steal some clothes. He seemed to be running low on joggers and small t-shirts.

I wonder where they all went?

Once she was done, he scooped her up in a bear hug making her laugh as he spun them round, narrowly missing smacking her head off the wall.

"You are crazy! You know that. You've brought a new level of stress and excitement into my life!" he dumped her on the sofa and knelt down next to her.

"You're a cop. I think the level of excitement we have been through is a little bit more extreme than most." Alex pointed out. She stopped talking when he looked like he was trying to express his feelings.

"I don't know what I would do if you stopped popping up at my doorstep. I wish you wouldn't just disappear." He said, lying across her with his weight making her laugh and squirm beneath him. "Marry me?" He hissed into her stomach. Alex stopped moving. He looked at her and grinned. She stared at him dumbfounded, questioning if he was serious. He held his breathe for the entire time as she started laughing.

"Of course not," she laughed, he fell on the floor looking dramatically devastated. "It would be a disaster." She stood up and tried to pull him off the ground with an arm. James scooted himself up on to his knees and held onto her wrist.

"Please, we could go to Vegas tonight?" James pleaded giving her the puppy dog eyes but his lips were quivering with laughter.

"Ask me another time when we both aren't drunk or sleep deprived." Alex offered but James made a comment that they were never in that sort of rational state around each other.

"You haven't given me a definitive answer!" James said looking sad. Alex had a different proposal in mind.

"The answer is no. I'm going back to bed." Alex sighed with a cheeky wink at him. "Do you want to join me to consummate the non-union?" She asked with a raised eye brow as he dropped her hand and stood up to stretch, the goofiness leaving his face.

"I would love to join you but I need to get a few hours of proper sleep before I go back into the precinct. This case is going to need as much experienced eyes looking at it as possible." He replied looking disappointed. Alex smiled and made her way back into the bedroom and collapse on to the bed. She Awoke up to him shaking her gently and saying that he had to go but she could stay as long as she needed. She thought she heard him propose again but she just ignored him completely, too comfortable to talk.

Poor guy, he didn't realise that with Alex comes Katy and I had no intention of being married to him. We were not exclusive.

Alex's phone woke her up a few hours later. She felt better but the vibrating seemed to go right through her. She rolled over and stretched an arm out for it on the bedside table. It was just a foot out of reach as she stretched her fingers for it. Then it stopped buzzing. The energy to check it seemed a little much for her so she just relaxed back onto the pillows and drifted for a moment. BUZZZZ. Alex let out an angry yell of frustration as it started ringing again. She grabbed it and pressed answer without looking at the screen.

"WHAT!" She yelled down the line.

"Hello Katy," said Walter's amused voice. "I take it that the plan went well then."

"What plan?" Alex sighed rolling onto her back with a grumble.

"The one to be spotted by Nicholas. He has left his gym and is going back to his apartment just now." He said, typing in the background as he accessed the CCTV network. "The president is issuing the arrest warrant today. We need to start taunting him a little."

"Oh shite." Alex gasped jumping out of bed. "Send me his address and I will get a cab there." Alex caught a look at herself in the mirror; she needed a shower. Not even the dampeners could hide the state she was in. "On second thoughts where will he be in an hour?" she asked.

Now You See Me, Now You Don't

Nicholas's view of Katy was going to have to be a fleeting glance. It needed to be visible on camera so he wouldn't think he had imagined it. Alex borrowed one of James's hoodies, her hair tied back beneath the hood. Nicholas was getting food from a Chinese restaurant. She wondered why he didn't get it delivered to his door but he seemed to enjoy walking around the city. Nicholas was always weird when it came to exercise. She stood by a lamppost across the road with an alley way she could escape down if needed.

Alex waited until he came out of the takeaway to turn off the dampeners. He stepped out of the door and held it open for the next person to go in with a friendly smile. Their eyes met across the street. He froze his expression shocked as Katy smiled at him. A lorry crossed their line of vision with perfect timing, she legged it through the alley; pulling off the hoodie and tossing it into a dumpster.

 Alex emerged at the other side of the alley; the dampeners on, her hair down and a dress unfurled to cover her jeans and she disappeared into the crowd of commuters. Nicholas came running out of the alley looking dazed; staring round, his phone out as he looked round. Alex let herself glance back; their eyes met but he was looking at a face that was thirty years older so his eyes kept searching. He ran down the road in the opposite direction as Alex flagged down a taxi. It seemed to be enough to for him to take the bait.

***

A week later

Alex was on a plane again. This time for a holiday; she had told James that she would be in Washington all week so he wouldn't bother her. The flight was long, into the heart of the Pacific landing on an island of Bora Bora where she was collected and driven off the tarmac to her hotel. The island was something from a fantasy book with crazy shaped mountains covered in rainforests, crystal blue water and clear skies. She had booked two bungalows at the resort; there was a special someone waiting there for her in the next bungalow was Rose and Elliot standing outside the entrance as she got off the buggy.

"You sly queen!" Rose exclaimed as they both squealed, jumped around as they greeted each other. "You send us boarding cards and instructions to pack for the beach. And then we turn up here?!" She asked, her voice reaching the ultrasonic octave.

"Well, I felt bad that you didn't get a proper honey moon and had to be in protection I thought this would be a good alternative." Alex laughed. Rose finally let go of her allowing her to greet Elliot. He scooped her up and swung her round in the biggest bear hug. She thought he was going to break some of her ribs.

"I would have got us a shared bungalow but then I thought that sharing with newlyweds would be a mistake." Alex explained as the porters had taken her bags into the bungalow. She gave a tip and we went into explore the interior; t had a pool overlooking the spectacular view of the ocean from the bedroom. Elliot and Rose started giggled as they admired the facilities. Alex wanted to check out the bedroom when their giggling intensified. Those two were so perfect for each other.

"What are you laughing at?" Alex asked pulling the door open to the bedroom. She let out a gasp in surprise being met with the most disturbing image; Josh was sprawled out on the bed with only a shell covering his privates and a rose in his mouth. There were rose petals laid around and champagne in a cool box. The other two glimpse the view and start cackling with laugher. Josh looking seductive face's contorted in equal shock and he fell out of the bed to grab one of the dressing gowns. Alex was dumbfounded.

"Oh my god, he went through with it you owe me fifty quid." Rose said and Elliot was on the floor crying with laughter. Josh slammed the door angrily.

"You look like such a tit." Elliot yelled through gasps escaping his chest.

"What is he doing here?" Alex asked in shock starting to laugh herself.

"We thought it might be nice for him to keep you company so we can have some alone time. We bought him a ticket when we found out. He's been a clingy pain in the arse since we got back. We had a bet on about what we could make him do when we got here." Rose replied gripping onto Elliot's shoulder for balance and whipping tears from her eyes with the other.

"What the hell are you two doing in here?" asked Josh covered in a dressing gown, barging through the bedroom door.

"Oh, just getting this." Elliot said and pulled out his phone to take a picture.

"That's it," yelled Josh, grabbing Elliot in a headlock and dragged him out of the back door. He hoisted him up and threw him into the sea. The splash sprayed the side of the bungalow. Alex blinked a few times at the sheer strength of the throw. Rose fearing for her safety took shelter behind Alex. "You're next," Josh threatened pointing at her.

He lunged for Rose who spun round Alex to remain safe. She wasn't getting in the middle of this so ducked out of the way to give Josh the change to grab her. Rose went over the side of the water into her husband's waiting arms with the loudest of screams. Josh cursed at the over the railing before turning round. Alex found the whole situation highly entertaining.

"Do you want to go in too?" Josh threatened her, more embarrassed than anything. Alex backed away with her hands up trying to stifle her laughter.

"I was laughing at them not you," she said passively backing away.

"You sure about that?" He asked, darting forward to try and grab her. Alex kept him at arm's length and notice Elliot sneaking in through the back door. She kept her eyes on Josh to keep his attention, he looked like he meant business.

"No, I'm supporting you, it was a lovely… surprise." Alex said just managing to keep a straight face as Elliot lunged at him and hauled him out onto the deck. She nearly had to crawl after them she was laughing so hard. Elliot had him by the neck and his arm behind his back. Josh dug his foot in so that Elliot couldn't get him out the door. Alex leant down to free it. "That's for not believing me." She smiled at him as Elliot pulled him closer to the edge.

"If I'm going the you are both coming with me!" He said and grabbed on to her wrist. His grip was unbreakable. On the edge of the deck, Josh pushed back with all his might that the three of them fell into the water. Alex let out a scream as they hit the water with a mighty splash. The water hit her hard on the back like falling onto concrete. She stroked out for the surface being dragged down by her dress. An arm linked around her waist, pulling her to the surface. She gasped from the shock as Josh swam them toward the ladder to the jetty.

Elliot and Rose scarpered back to their bungalow. Josh helped Alex get out of the water. She had housekeeping come to collect their clothes to try and salvage them. Her back hurt from the impact of the water which she tried to hide. Josh could tell that she was annoyed at her so didn't push it and stayed outside while she changed.

After the clothes were collected, she went to the back door and pulled the curtain back. Josh was dripping wet still in his dressing gown with her salvaged shoe in his hand looking sorry. He mouthed it's cold through the window and just looked really pathetic. Alex grimaced and let him in. He stepped inside in his sopping wet dressing gown and held the shoe out to her. She took it and threw it across the room.

"Don't you dare go anywhere in that disgusting gown." Alex advised him with a small smile.

"Ok," he replied and let it drop to the ground leaving him completely naked. Alex winked at him and walked away towards the bedroom leaving her dressing gown at the door. Josh pulled the curtain shut before following her in.

Should I feel guilty about spending time with him again? It wasn't like me and James were together officially. What the hell….

The week started off with them going snorkelling through the coral reefs off round the edge of the islands. There were giant manta rays and turtles feeding off the reef. The coral colours were incredible. Alex had read somewhere that the snorkelling was one of the best in the world. The water was warm and crystal clear. She wasn't very fast swimmer even with her flippers so Josh grabbed her hand and towed her alongside to see some of the deeper reefs.

They hired a private yacht to take them on a cruise around the island and get a little bit of local history. They could dive down to the tikis left by an artist to remember the old religion of the island before the Christian converts arrived. Afterwards, they were taken back to the resort to the restaurants and splurged on the most wonderful drinks and food. Rose and Alex came up with a plan, winding the guys up for an exciting night which actually involved all four of them curled up on the couch watching Moana. It became a sing along and more drinks later the boys joined in.

As it was the full moon tonight, everything was bathed in a beautiful silver light. This called for skinny dipping and swimming in the water. But as soon as there was the first sign of reef sharks Rose and Alex scarpered back to the bungalows. Despite the exciting day, they were all very tired. Alex had kicked Josh out onto the deck so that she could have a little bit of peace. Yet he ended up on doorstep as the other two abandoned him to have "honey moon time" as they put it. Alex answered the door with her hand on her hip ready to make him sleep outside.

"Please can I join you. The wood is so uncomfortable. I've come all this way too see you surely we can just share as friends." He asked trying the pathetic expression again. Alex rolled her eyes at him but he had already won her over.

"Fine, but you sleep on the couch. I want the bed to myself." Alex ordered him, pointing with her finger as he slipped in through the door way. He shut the door behind him with a wicked smile and a glint in his eye. *Oh no.* He grabbed Alex and pulled her into a fireman's lift before she could protest.

For a second, she thought he was going to put her back in the sea as we head towards the deck. "Don't you dare!" Alex warned, squirming in his arms. He gave her a hard smack on the arse and walked into the bedroom instead and depositing her onto the floor.

"The bed is mine," Josh declared, with a leap in the air he starfished on top of it. Alex jumped up, pushing him off the mattress with her feet. He pulled the whole cover off with him. "You may have the mattress but I'm keeping the essence of it," He declared wrapping the duvet round him like a cape, taring out of the room. Alex took chase yelling at the weirdo. She trapped him in the bathroom, retrieved the duvet and returned to the bed. It only escalated from there.

The fight for the bed started and turned into something else; hot and primal. Both were equally as competitive and deadly trained. It wasn't a fair match; but who for? The next morning, they are joined by Rose and Elliot for breakfast, they looked a little worse for wear.

"What are those bruises on your arm?" asked Rose as their food was delivered.

"Nothing." Alex replied rather quickly helping herself to juice.

"Why have you got a tinge of a black eye?" Rose asked Josh instead. He looked away and didn't answer. *Before you ask no I did not hit him, he injured himself...* The memory made Alex snort into her glass sending juice up her nose. Rose and Elliot looked at each other and decided not to ask.

The time passed all too quickly and before you know it, Alex had to get on a flight back to America. She had paid for Rose and Elliot to stay on another week and have a proper honey moon by themselves. Josh was going back to the UK. He offered to come and work for Alex instead of going back into witness protection but the whole situation was too complicated. Plus, if Alex had someone working for her who had been together with intimately it might be a conflict of interest so she sent him home.

Alex was very fond of Josh but that was all she felt towards him. He made her laugh and smile and let her just be herself and that's what she needed. It was refreshing and the best protection be could offer her to keep their antics to himself as she went back to the job. It made her realise that her heart might be fonder for James than she realised. She looked forward to returning home. After a teary goodbye and the promise to fulfil her vow to return once the mission was up, they made their goodbyes.

The flight back was comfortable however the crossing over the time zones on the flight home so she had a worse jet lag than she had coming back from China. Alex had a day to herself in the apartment to organise and sleep. She had a lovely golden tan which she wanted to show off but there wasn't much she could do except wear running shorts and sports bra out jogging. Nicholas was going to get another sighting before he went out on a complex mission in the middle east. He would be gone for several months.

This was the next glimpse he had to catch off her before he left. The arrest warrant hadn't found the presidents Cover Girl but as the situation with the conflicts between China and Russia escalated with links to the American President came to light the search would increase and Nicholas would be called back. But it would take some time.

Walter told her that he was in the park. What he failed to mention was that Nicholas was on a date. The woman was stunning; tall, tanned, toned and blonde. Alex watched them for a second from around the corner. He looked happy. There was a pang of irritation. Who could she be? Was Alex jealous? It had been a long time he was allowed to live his life? She gritted her teeth. Sent Walter the signal from her watch and turned off the dampener. Alex started jogging past; ensuring that she was within his eye line. There was a group of joggers ahead she could lose him in if he took chase again. He didn't even look up he was more focused on his date.

Alex tried running past several times and the smarmy bastard didn't even have the decency to look up. She needed to take a new tactic. Alex ran straight past them and pretended to fall over with a shriek. She actually fell, there was no need to pretend. She pushed herself up on her hands, her hair around her face and looked at them. They were both staring at her. This time Alex and Nicholas made eye contact. His expression dropped. He got to his feet.

Shite. Alex realised he knew it was her this time. She ran. So hard. So fast. The dampeners were on but Nicholas was behind her. She gasped for breath as he pursued her, no group to hide in. The road started to rise. He was making up the ground as she slowed down. Alex dived between two crossing horse and carts running for the bus instead.

"Katy, straight ahead run into the crowd." Walter instructed as Alex kept pushing through the branches and came out into a throng of tourists. She ran amongst them and stooped down. Her heart pounding, her face glowing with the effort. The adrenaline surged through her as she tried to control her breathing.

Nicholas was ten seconds behind but there was woman dressed like Alex walking in different directions. Walter had this planned just in case. Alex tried to control her breathing and walk away slowly. The dampeners were on. Nicholas was checking all the women running in between them individually. He approached Alex and spun her round.

For the first time in months, we were looking each other in the eye. Alex tried to look affronted as his eyes studied her face. Alex heart thumped thought for a second that the dampeners weren't working. The heat radiated off her. Surely, he could feel the sweat and throbbing of her pulse on her skin. Then he let her go and moved onto the next woman. Alex kept walking until she caught her breathe and then ran straight back to her apartment. That had been way too close.

Could he have thought that he was just seeing Alex everywhere and doubting himself. There wasn't any video footage so when he went through it or asked Walter too there was no way that he would have seen her. The plan was set now only time would tell in the order in which the next events played out.

But you know what happened next...

Nicholas

It was months later. Nicholas had been working on his own. Things were getting darker by the day. Russia and China were threatening to launch nuclear attacks on each other. There had already been cyber-attacks bringing down their transport and medical networks. People were scared but America was in its element sending aid, creating trade talks and sanctions. The economy was booming and the shares were soaring as America became the economic centre of the world while the rest self-destructed. Yet he had been focused on one thing. Finding Katy Jones.

There were dozens of stories of Cover Girls operating around the world. Erin Defraz had been cleared off all charged but her network had been remotely accessed by a Chinese mob group which were hacking the governments system. This had been stopped but the skill in pulling off the negotiation could only have been pulled off by the real Cover Girl. The image dampener traces were so scattered. There was one present in beginning. It that was around the time that Erin had been present for the global leader's conference in Beijing. The rest of the president's staff had been there. It was all linked to the patterns laid out for them. He knew the answer was staring him in the face. He couldn't see it. Katy's voice spoke to him in his dreams telling him to look harder.

The man who he had saw Katy with had been the police captain who worked in the downtown precinct. Though Katy had been with him that day, the man himself was a little bit of a player known for having women entering and leaving his apartment. He had been invoiced with a spunky girl from the New York senator's office. But she had lost her job and moved away when her flat burned down so she had been ruled out. Katy had left a trail of bread crumbs for him although he didn't know where they lead. He had seen her too; in the park and on the street. Not just in the cameras, at least he thought. Every time he went out, he looked for her.

"I just don't understand how she pulled all of this off on her own?" Nicholas asked Walter one day in the office. The whole thing was giving him a headache and the president's office was pressing for her arrest by the end of the week. "How could she have faked her own death, got to the president and resided on her own for this long?"

"It doesn't make sense." replied Walter looking equally as tired as he ran his hands through his wild hair. He had been at her side this whole-time analysing data and trolling through endless footage of where the dampeners were traced. The effort was taking their toll on everyone in the department. The power of the pentagon couldn't find her, someone had to be helping her. She had so many connections in the crime world they needed time to work out who.

The majority of the scans had been around Washington but any movements of Miss Defraz had been ruled out to narrow down the search. "The president is concerned that there was a woman claiming to be the Cover Girl operating in Moscow a few days after being traced on American soil."

"Why, why is the president so keen on bringing her in?" Nicholas questioned. "We can't prove that he is guilty until we find something concrete. Could we offer Katy a deal for talking to us. There must be away to contact her."

"You know she won't risk anything. But what could make her come to you voluntarily that could just give us enough time to ask her some questions." Walter suggested. He didn't know her that well yet the man worked with numbers and statistics and could make accurate predictions about behaviours for most people except her.

"I would need to be in some serious danger or maybe I could do something so extreme that she would come." Nicholas started to think deep about what had been her drive. So far Katy had nothing to lose but hadn't it away been Alex was the side of herself which she protected. It was a long shot but it might be worth a try to bring her out of the shadows.

***

Walter sent out a message on the dark web. To find the heir of the Belize fortune the information would be shared to the internet; profile, diary details, banking information. This would be shared to everyone good and bad revealing the source of her income which they had deduced how she managed to support herself after all of this time. It would be shared at midnight unless she contacted him to find a time to meet. It took two days but then there was a message coming through.

"You bastard, meet me at the place where you close the door."

"Where does she mean?" Walter asked trying different cyphers on the message. Nicholas knew where she meant. The café where they had met all that time ago after he had moved to New York to escape his grief. He was to go alone, no one else in the department knew of the plan. That was the deal just me and her for old times. He walked down the street feeling the empty void of sadness he had felt last time. The street was deserted except for the small coffee shop. Even in the cold weather there were tables outside. Four women sat in the chairs.

Nicholas looked at them all and sat down in the only empty table. The waitress came out and poured him some coffee but didn't bother him again. Three of the women got up at the same time and walked away leaving him and one other alone. Nicholas glanced round and noticed he was back-to-back with the last woman.

"Hey Nick," said an unfamiliar voice. "It's been a long time hasn't it." Of course, she was wearing a voice chip.

"It sure has and you have been up to some trouble, haven't you?" Nicholas asked, taking a sip of his coffee.

"I've been busy, you could say that. I notice that you have been following the copy cats. Surely you know that I have so much more potential than just mediocre crimes." She replied, hearing the clink of her mug as she put it down.

"You are wanted by the President. If I were to follow my oath, I would bring you in right now. It's for the sake of our friendship that I am giving you a chance to speak." Nicholas said and waited for her response.

"If you had done your research, you would have already discovered what was going on. Do I need to spell it out for you?" she asked him and he hear the familiar sarcasm in her voice. The accent was so different but the woman he knew was still there. This was Katy he was talking too. He needed to get to Alex.

"Tell me what happened and I can help you." He insisted turning round to look her in the eye. Perhaps he could take her dampeners off.

"Sorry it's *client privilege*." Katy emphasized the phrase. "But please look harder and you can find out for yourself." She warned standing up and then turned to look at him. "I miss you," she added her voice softening. She touched a finger to her neck and the dampener turned off so he could look into her eyes. The eyes he saw in his nightmares, staring up at him through the rubble. Her smiled softened him and it was just like old times with his friend after everything they had been through together. The instinct to protect her was just as strong as ever. His com makes a rattling sound. Walter was trying to get through.

"I have to go." She said, turning her dampener back on to show a different face this time. Her expression froze as she listened to something in her ear looking concerned. She stood up abruptly, turning to him with a panicked expression.

 "Help Walter!" She instructed him; her eyes wide. He knew something had happened.

"What?" Nicholas asked, his heart rate rising. Before she could answer there was a shot fired and she froze in front of him as a taser caught her off guard. She yelled out in pain and fell to the ground as the electric current surges through her. Nicholas knelt beside her gripping her hand as she shook. They were surrounded by police surging around them, Brady walking in amongst them.

"Good work Castle, you caught her." She said, looking down at Katy. "Get the dampeners off her." Nicholas reached down to her neck he couldn't feel or see them even at the spot that Katy just touched.

"I can't," He replied, searching both sides beneath her hair, "I've never seen tech like this." The corners of her mouth curved in a small smile as she shuddered beneath him.

"That's because Walter has been helping her. I caught him in a secret room talking to her. He took me out and fled. He has been covering her tracks this whole time. But we have her. The president will be pleased. Cuff her and take her to the nearest precinct to be interviewed. I want this done quietly," she said to one of the officers who had cuffed Katy and pulled her to her feet.

"Come on Brady, don't be a stickler for the rules. You know there is more to this than meets the eye." Katy said to her as she was hauled away. Brady ignored her and gave more instructions to the police officers. Nicholas and Katy looked at each other before she was taken away. Silently she told him. "Keep your eyes open."

Let Me Tell You How It Is

Katy

Katy was locked in a cell somewhere in the city. She had been taken away in a van with blackened out windows. They drove for a while. She didn't have her phone. Walter had been compromised. She didn't know where he was. But her dampeners were operating. Walter had done such a good job designing them so her face would remain anonymous and the boss would have a trace on her. Would they be able to break into them? Time went on. Katy was given basic food but that was all the interactions she had. Then the door opened as she dosed off. Nicholas came in. He had a pair of cuffs and placed them on her hands leading her out of the cell.

We did not make eye contact; she couldn't give him any information. Alex was taken into an interrogation room and her hands were cuffed to the table.

"Really?" Katy asked, rattling the cuff at him. "What do you expect me to do, break down the wall or knock you out!" He didn't reply and left her alone in the room. Was he being kept on the case for his professionalism or that he knew her patterns and weaknesses if she tried to trick them? *Hah, they wished!*

She had to wait several more minutes. The chain on the cuffs is long that Katy able to move around. They had one of the one-way mirrors. Katy could tell she was being observed, she had been trained to resist interrogation. Katy smiled and waved at the people in the mirror. It was pretty boring after five minutes. She put her feet up on the desk and start twiddling her thumbs.

The person who walked through that door was not who she expected.

Captain James. He looked directly at her. She remembered that the dampeners were programmed to let him see her true face. She couldn't reprogramme them without her phone. They didn't know this though so she had to keep this information a secret.

"It's just you and me. This is your chance to tell me what has happened. What have you gotten involved in? Your face is on the wanted poster for one of the most wanted women in the country." Katy hesitated looking down at her fingers as her feeling surfaced. Her heart beat to tell him the truth but she had to supress Alex. Katy would save them all. It was the ultimate test. "Tell me now and I can try to help you." Katy reached out for his hand but he took his off the table.

"My name isn't Alex, it's actually Katy Jones. Well really, it's Alex but I have two names. The person you got to know over our time together was Alex." Katy started to explain as she reached up and press the button against her neck. The image dampener was finger print activated. No one else had worked it out yet. Her voice went back to normal. "I'm from London." Alex explained as her voice switched back to her English accent. He looked shocked by the change. "I am the world-renowned Cover Girl and this is my confession. I was hired by a client in America. I have been working for several months to get noticed by the President of the United States. He hired me to plant a bug on the Russian president and drive a wedge between China and Russia to remove the threat from the US soils and let the economy grow while a war raged on and he would never be identified as the perpetrator."

"But what he didn't count on was that while his contract was fulfilled. The bug system scrambled the information and he discovered that there was a botched job. After I refused to give his money back and complete the task. I've been visiting different mafias and countries to get his attention but I have never delved any information to any of the USA's enemies or endangered any lives." She could feel everyone listening to the information. "All this time I recorded the information and right now, after my arrest it has been shared on social media for the country and world to see." Alex explained leaning back on her chair, this was the final part of the plan that had been initiated by Walter in her ear and the boss had taken over control of the system. James stared at her in silence for a minute. There was a buzzing over the radio.

"Yes, that will be the new breaking out over social media and in about thirty seconds there is going to be a call coming in from the president to have me brought into the pentagon." Katy gestured to the radio for him to listen. "But here is the choice you have to make. You have read my file; you know I don't know anything about the crime or confess. I have broken the rules. That was part of my contract now my end if fulfilled I am free to live my life. If you want to turn me over to the dirty president, be my guest. You know me. You know I wouldn't be here if I didn't think it was the right thing to do." Katy explained, everything had been planned out. Her job was finished and now she was on her own. Her life was in his hands. This time there was no back up plan or protection.

James walked out of the room and left alone. Katy caught a glimpse of the turmoil going on outside. *You would think that the room was sound proof but she could hear the arguments.* That was without the dampener; she could tap into the radio waves, phone lines and WIFI calls. This dampener had so many features. Her watch also received a message. She kept it hidden in her bra, luckily didn't set of the detectors. There was a message from the director.

"Mission complete. You have done a great service to the country. I know the cost of you coming forward has had. That was an unfortunate turn of events. Time to disappear again. Yours, Former President Scott."

Yes, I can confirm that the man who hired me all those months ago was the former president. I witnessed an altercation you see after the events in Paris. There was a security meeting held by the global leaders. On a visit to the MI5 office, I was walking down the corridor to a meeting room where two men were arguing. There was no one else around. The voices drew me in so I paused outside of the door, my image dampeners were off.

"You will never get away with this. The people will not stand for it!" came the familiar voice.

"Your time is over Scott. I will take control and sort this country out." The future president said.

"The people will never vote for you!" Scott claimed.

"The people don't have a say. They are just sheep looking for a leader, if I spurted some words from Hitler, they would follow me and not think for themselves. By any means my new friends in Russia will be dealing with this for me. Just you watch! I will take this country back to the time when we were rich, respected and feared!" The future president declared and then headed for the door. I darted up the corridor and kept walking. He passed me and looked directly at my face suspiciously. I smiled and kept walking, waiting for him to disappear before I sneaked into the meeting room.

President Scott was staring out of the window at the river Thames thinking hard to himself. The elections were very soon and he was going to be forced out of office. I was still waiting to be placed into protective custody so I had been roaming the building for the past few days since my discharge from hospital.

"Excuse me sir. My name is Katy Jones, I just overheard what was said," I tried to introduce herself but he didn't turn round to acknowledge me.

"Then you will be one of the only people in the world that will believe me that America is heading for some dark times with that man. There is nothing that can stop him." He said sounding defeated.

"I think I can help you there. Let me tell you a little about what I do." I said and I described my role and what had been happening over the past couple of months.

"That was you?" He said looking me up and down once I had finished my story. "Saving Monaco, reducing the drug traffic from Belize. You look so normal; how could you attain such amazing feats?" He asked.

"By doing my job." I replied and I could see in his mind that he was formulating a plan.

"Are you currently working on anything right now?" He asked. I shook my head in reply.

"Excellent well I want to hire you but as he just saw you and you have a reputation; we need to make you disappear..."

***

Alex pulled herself out of the memory of the encounter that changed everything as James walked back into the room. She slid the watch into her bra. He shut the door behind him and turned off the cameras in the room. He came over to the table and uncuffed her.

"You need to get out of here. The president has sent in a hit squad to bring you to him." He said as he released her hands. "Nicholas will get you out but we need to make this look convincing." He pulled out his fire arm and fired it in the air making her flinch. "Use the end of the gun to hit me!" He ordered. Alex hesitated but he pushed it into her hands. They're eyes met; she knew right then he might be the one to come back for.

First, she pulled him into a kiss. For a second, the danger, the drama drove them wild as their fingers grasped at each other. Alex pulled her arm back and hit him as hard over the head as she could. James fell to the ground bleeding. Alex lowered him to the ground so he wouldn't hit his head as the cameras came back on.   She ran out of the door. Nicholas was standing outside.

"Come with me." He said holding out his hand like old times. Katy smiled at him.

"I'm sorry I had to trick you but it's over now." Katy said, he pulled her along as ran towards the stair case. Instead of going down the stairs they went up to the roof. There was a helicopter sat on the helipad. They ran to it, climbing into the front seats. She buckled herself in as Nicholas started up the engine and the rotors started to turn.

"How on earth do you know how to fly this?" Alex yelled as the helicopter lifted off the pad. There was a clank as bullets hit the metal doors.

"It's been a while since you last saw me." Nick replied grinning and handed her a gun. "Give'em hell." He instructed; Alex fired back at the agents. Nicholas got the power up and lifted us off the pad. "I've missed this! Me and you against the world." They didn't rise into the air but moved to the side of the building and plummeted down. The roasters spun yet they were freefalling.

Alex screamed clinging on to the chair for dear life. Then Nick pulled the toggle, levelling out over the road and flew low between the buildings. He grabbed her hand to reassure her. "They won't fire down off the building in case they hit civilians."

They weaved through the buildings until we reached the river starting to climb and followed the water along the coast. Nicholas wasn't counting on the fighter jet coming in behind them. They cleared the city and followed the coast north being pursued by the jet. Nicholas dodged the shots fired however there was only so much manoeuvring that could be done in the helicopter. BANG! The tail was hit sending the dials into haywire and setting alarms off. Nicholas instructed Alex to brace as they spun toward the surface of the sea. They hit the surface hard as the jet shot over head.

Every second count, the helmet stopped the worse of the impact. Alex pulled at the clips on her seat belt to free herself as the helicopter started to sink. Except Nicholas seemed dazed. She reached over, managed to get his clips undone as they opened the door. He came too as the cabin filled with water. Together hand in hand, they struck out towards the surface.

A missile hit the surface of the water close to them exploding around them. The heat shot out, the force of the water. All sense of direction was lost as the heat and forces propelled them away and, in the confusion, Alex lost her grip on Nicholas's hand. She spun through the bubbles, panic coursing through her. It took all her self-control to not open her mouth. Alex gasped at the surface for air before a second missile hit the water.

***

Alex awoke cold and spluttering. She was on dry land or at least, she was on the edge of the water. Her side hurt and there was a horrible gash on her arm. She rolled over and looked behind her to see Nicholas unconscious with his hand next to her. Alex scrambled up beside him, putting a finger to his neck. There was a pulse but it was weak. He must have dragged her out of the water. She had no idea how. Alex pulled out the watch which thankfully was waterproof and found their location. They were miles away from anywhere. The watch sputtered and died. She threw it into the water in annoyance.

Whatever was happening she knew they were too exposed. Alex grabbed both of Nick's arms and dragged him up the beach. He was such a dead weight she could only get a few yards. There was a broken log close by. I pulled him over to it and propped him up high enough she could get his weight over her shoulders. Despite the pain, she found the strength to haul him up and start walking. They took shelter in the trees; the priority was to find fresh water.

Alex could hear helicopters in the distance but she didn't know how far away they were. Who knows where the tide had taken them? They were extremely lucky the water was so warm but she was feeling cold. Starting a fire would be stupid instead Alex just huddled close to Nicholas for heat. They had a long night. She drifted in and out of sleep. The pain in her side was getting worse throughout.

Alex awoke to movement next to her. Her temperature was creeping up making her sweat despite the chill of the night. Nicholas had woken up. He seemed confused at how they had come to be in the woods. He sat up and moved the hair away from her face.

"Alex you're burning up!" he said and then pulled the shirt up to reveal her side. He blanched and then tried to keep a neutral expression.

"How bad is it?" Alex asked, whipping away the sweat falling into her eyes.

"You will be fine." He lied and she could see the fear in his eyes. "How did we get off the beach?"

"I carried you," Alex said. He laughed as if she were joking then looked impressed.

"I guess were even, I had to pull your arse out of the water. I don't know how long I swam for. You wouldn't keep your head above water." He paused, looking around them.

"Well let's get going." Alex said trying to stand up. She pushed her hand against a tree to stop herself wobbling. Nicholas looked anxiously around them.

"You won't be walking anywhere." He stooped down, pulling her over his shoulders. "We need to get some help and I'm faster than you." He started jogging and following the dawn light to find south through the trees. Alex drifted in and out of consciousness. They stopped at a stream to have a drink but other than that, they kept going until Nicholas stopped to look at something in the mud. He placed Alex on her feet next to him in the long grass, her hand on his shoulder for balance. Her head spun being upright; feeling worse by the second.

"There is a search party in the trees. I don't know who they are." Nicholas thought out loud, examining the prints. Alex didn't hear him as she fainted. He caught her before she fell hard; her temperature was up, her breathing light and her pulse rapid. He checked her injury that was turning black; a sure sign of infection. He tried to wrap it but she suddenly gasped and stopped breathing.

"Don't you dare, not when I just got you back."

He bent over her, opening her mouth to force air into her lungs. *I was told later I had been suffocating from delayed water inhalation.* Noise came from over head as he gave her chest compressions and breathes until she stirred uncomfortably and took a breath in, spluttering. She coughed up a couple of mouthfuls of water. Alex opened her eyes to see him nose to nose.

"Don't do that again." Nicholas nearly growled at her as the yelling was got closer. There was a racket as a helicopter flew overhead. "Crap, they might have thermal imagine cameras. Stay here!" He ordered and ran off into the woods. The helicopter followed him leaving Alex alone hidden between some bushes. The sound got louder as people followed and then there were screams as Nick was captured. God knows by who. Alex lay there listening. She concentrated on her breathing as the pain in her side intensified. Even lifting her head made it spin. She needed medical attention.

There was a crack of a branch behind her. She turned over and see a pair of eyes staring at her. From the ground all she could see was a big white set of teeth and as the animal sniffed her. She thought she saw someone she knew next to her. Someone pushed in at her side. Alex felt the pain in her side sear again and she blacked out once more as torches shone on her face. Her instinct to run was gone. Whoever it was; she needed help.

***

Alex had faint memories of teams of masked men surrounding them; shouts, yells, barking. They had attempted to question her however there was no choice except to attend to her wound. The ambulance was pulled over and they were switched into a secure vehicle.

There were medical machines around her attached to her aching side. She opened her eyes weakly and looked around the room. James was sat in one chair and Nicholas in another. Both were fast asleep. Alex felt her legs were really heavy. There were several blankets draped over her. She tried to sit up in bed, crinkling the foil that had been placed around her causing Nicholas and James both woke up with a jolt.

"Hello," Alex said gruffly, her voice rough. Nicholas crushed her in his arms, she could feel the relief that she was awake. Alex reached out with her free hand to grasp James's too. He looked exhausted, his uniform all out of place and a large bruise on the side of his face. "Where are we? What happened?" she asked, her voice sounding croaky and dry.

"James found us. The dog team was sent out after the drones spotted us. The truth came out and you were officially exonerated of all charges. But our van was intercepted; the president had ordered it to be diverted to him. He's going down and the vice president is taking emergency powers. The impeachment trial is being held right now. Russia and China have declared a cease fire. Walter managed to divert the van to the safe house and from there we were transferred back into the city. The former President was able to pull some strings that saved our lives before he goes underground. He cannot be associated with this mission." Nicholas explained sitting back as James poured her some water. It was over, they were safe.

Someone moved in the door way, Alex saw Walter waiting in the background. He pushed his glasses up his nose and smiled awkwardly at her. Alex opened her harms for him to hug her; he was her true friend this whole time.

"Are Rose, Elliot and Josh, ok?" Alex asked letting go of Walter and taking a long drink of water.

"Yes, they are still in witness protection but they can go back to their normal lives once everything has died down." Walter explained, pulling a tablet off the table and typing away. "Rose has promised to use her own alter ego and not the Cover Girl anymore for her own safety." He continued and everyone in the room shared a look of concern.

"What's wrong?" Alex asked as they finished exchanging glances. Something had been decided while she was asleep.

"Katy needs to retire for good." Nicholas started to explain. "You breeched your contract; your motivations, movements, strategies and dampener disguises were all exposed on the dark web by the president. You reputation is in tatters and there are a lot of people after you." He finished looking sad. "Walter has hidden your wealth well and it will continue to support you but any word of the Cover Girl operating again and you will likely to be killed. The president has ruined any chance of you working again. An eye for an eye as he put it."

"So, what am I meant to do then?" Alex asked, feeling her soul crack, sinking back into bed. *I was speechless. Nothing sassy to reply.*

"Well, you can choose somewhere and live a normal life; take your fortune and spend your days in amazing places or build a business empire. Or you could have a simple and safe life with me." James said, squeezing her hand tight, running his hand over the side of her face. Her stomach twisted slightly. "I have a ranch that belonged to my family out in Wyoming, no signal, no neighbours for miles. We could just disappear and live there happily." Alex blinked at him without replying. She didn't have the heart to tell him how terribly boring it sounded.

Remind me to send a copy of He's just not that into you.

"On the other hand, we could give it some time and you could come and work for the MI5 again. I want to transfer back to the UK and I could take you with me. Walter is going to be reinstated with a full investigation and pardon for services to the country. He can get you home. It won't be like it was but we can work together again and lead the live you have been wanting back after all this time?" Nicholas offered. Both of them seemed to be trying to sell each option to her. It was like the world had been closed to her. Two lives she never wanted despite a taste of each.

*What do you think? *

Sorry girl, I'm not going to be able to call the shots anymore. It's your turn to take care of us. Just make a good decision.

*Ok, stay with me. *

Always.

For once it seemed that Alex was going to make the shots; no conflict, no inner voice or other persona. With a deep breathe she put Katy in a box, pushed it into the depth of her mind, somewhere quiet and dark. Alex felt the silence in her heart. It was strange, feeling oddly alone, her choices were her own and no one else's except from the two offers in front of her. Or just maybe there was another way….

"I choose" …

Hang on,

Wait a minute.

You just shut me out?!

After everything we have done for this country.

I under the threat but do you really thing that this is the end of my story. She could just let go of me after all of this time. I might not be as loud but I will always be here watching and judging.

For now, this is the right thing to do? Keep everyone in the dark, let the world reset and the danger fade. Oh, but you know how much I like to live on the side of danger. This is not over.

How long do you think she could keep me away? Oh, Alex my dear, Nicholas my friend, James my hhmmm I wouldn't say love but you are useful. We had fun.

I will be back.

I will rise again.

The Cover Girl will never be stopped.

You are just going to have to wait and find out.

All my love,

Katy Jones.

www.ingramcontent.com/pod-product-compliance
Lightning Source LLC
Chambersburg PA
CBHW050330160726

48002CB00001B/253